BETRAYAL!

"What does your employer want from me?" Anastasia Keresnky asked the mercenary.

"*From* you?" the woman replied. "Nothing. In fact, my employer wants to help you achieve your goals."

"How?"

"By offering you the assistance of a unit or more of trusted mercenaries, including artillery, battle armor, and 'Mechs."

Anastasia stiffened. "Please convey my thanks to your employer, and let him know that my Wolves and I do not desire mercenary assistance at the present time."

"Is that your last word on the subject?"

"It is my only word."

The other woman shrugged. "Whatever you say. But the offer remains open." Then she gave Anastasia a level look. "And a word of advice from me to you, purely out of the kindness of my heart—"

Anastasia was still offended. "Yes?"

"Clean up your own house before somebody outside cleans it for you. How do you think we got your secret frequency?"

D0018559

MECHWARRIOR
DARK AGE

TRUTH AND SHADOWS

A BATTLETECH® NOVEL

Martin Delrio

A ROC BOOK

ROC
Published by New American Library, a division of
Penguin Group (USA) Inc., 375 Hudson Street,
New York, New York 10014, U.S.A.
Penguin Books Ltd, 80 Strand,
London WC2R 0RL, England
Penguin Books Australia Ltd, 250 Camberwell Road,
Camberwell, Victoria 3124, Australia
Penguin Books Canada Ltd, 10 Alcorn Avenue,
Toronto, Ontario, Canada M4V 3B2
Penguin Books (N.Z.) Ltd, Cnr Rosedale and Airborne Roads,
Albany, Auckland 1310, New Zealand

Penguin Books Ltd, Registered Offices:
80 Strand, London WC2R 0RL, England

First published by Roc, an imprint of New American Library,
a division of Penguin Group (USA) Inc.

First Printing, August 2003
10 9 8 7 6 5 4 3 2 1

THE INNER SPHERE

REPUBLIC TERRITORY

AD SECURITAS PER UNITAS · REPUBLIC OF THE SPHERE ·

REPUBLIC OF THE SPHERE

PREFECTURES I, III, IV AND V

PREFECTURES OF THE REPUBLIC

I II III IV V VI VII VIII IX X

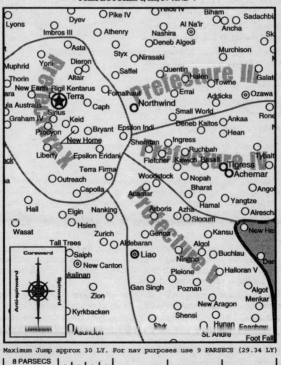

Lyons · Dyev · Pike IV · Telos IV · Biham · Sadachbia
Imbros III · Athenry · Nashira · Ancha · Sk
Asta · Deneb Algedi · Murchison
Muphrid · Yorii · Dieron · Styx · Nirasaki
Thorin · Altair · Saffel · Quentin · Halen · Towne · Galati
New Earth · Rigil Kentarus · Fomalhaut · Errai · Addicks · Ozawa
ara · Terra · Caph · Northwind · Small World · Ankaa · Rone
ula Australis · Sirius · Keid · Epsilon Indi · Deneb Kaitos · Hean
Graham IV · Procyon · Bryant · Sheratan · Ingress · Ruchbah
Liberty · New Home · Fletcher · Kawich · Basalt · Tybalt
ock · Epsilon Eridani · Tigress · Achernar
Terra Firma · Woodstock · Nopah · Ango
Outreach · Acamar · Bharat · Yangtze
Capolla · Arboris · Azha · Hamal · Alresch
Hall · Elgin · Nanking · Slocum
Wasat · Hsien · Zurich · Genoa · Kansu · New He
Tall Trees · Aldebaran · Algol · Buchlau · Dar
Saiph · Liao · Ningpo · Halloran V
New Canton · Pleione · Algot
kalinan · Gan Singh · Poznan · Menkar
Zion · New Aragon
Kyrkbacken · Shensi
Asuncion · Shir · Hunan · Eaghow
St. Andre · Foot Fall

Prefecture I

Prefecture III

Prefecture IV

Prefecture V

Coreward
Anti-spinward · Spinward
Rimward

Maximum Jump approx 30 LY. For nav purposes use 9 PARSECS (29.34 LY)

8 PARSECS

40 PARSECS OR 130.4 LIGHT YEARS

PART ONE

Lurking
November–December 3133

1

*Balfour-Douglas Petrochemicals Offshore Drilling
Station #47
Oilfields Coast, Northwind
Prefecture III, The Republic of the Sphere
November 3133; dry season*

Ian Murchison, resident medic on Balfour-Douglas's
Station #47, leaned on the rail of the oil rig's observation deck, watching the night sky and taking his ease
after a long day. Here on Kearney's Oilfields Coast,
the low latitude made for warm weather despite the
season. The continental landmass was a dark bulk
away over the water to the east, and the memory of
sunset lingered in a purple glow along the seaward
horizon.

There was no moon tonight to overpower the rest

of the night sky. Murchison had seen a meteor shower the night before, out of the usual time for such—maybe, he'd speculated, bits of the tail of some minor and uncharted comet, making its long elliptical journey around Northwind system's central star, only brushing atmosphere once out of centuries. Tonight, however, he saw nothing but the regular twinkling stars, their light refracted by the humid ocean air.

Today had been a long day, but a dull one. Murchison hadn't minded; in his opinion, a little dullness now and then was a good thing. Out on an oil rig, days that weren't dull tended to involve nasty industrial accidents or sudden illnesses, and Balfour-Douglas #47 was a long way from a good hospital, on a long empty stretch of coastline. Even a VTOL craft summoned to evacuate someone seriously ill or injured had to come from more than three hours away—which meant that in most emergencies, Murchison's patient was either dead or stable long before transport arrived. Balfour-Douglas #47 hadn't had one of those emergencies since Barry O'Mara's appendix went bad on him in the middle of a force 10 storm, and Murchison was in no hurry to experience another one soon.

He pushed away from the rail. He'd dawdled out here enjoying the night air long enough. It was time to go back to his office cubby, write up the log of the day's cuts and scrapes and bruises, lock up all the drawers and cabinets, and go to bed. If any pain or discomfort decided to manifest itself later, someone would wake him.

A faint sound—the clink of metal against metal—broke the night. Murchison knew all the regular sounds of the oil rig, so that his mind erased them without thinking all day and night and let him read their steady underbeat as silence, but this sound had not been one of the regular noises. He paused, listening, but heard no repetition of the metallic clink.

He shrugged. Maybe somebody on another of the platform's several decks had dropped something; sounds carried out here on the water, and the clinking noise could have come from anywhere on the rig. Or maybe the sound had been the metallic structure of the platform itself flexing and creaking, which meant that in a day or two something on the rig would break, probably without warning, and Murchison would have to patch up whoever was in the way when it went.

Whatever, he thought. There was nothing he could do about any of it tonight. He continued on his way inside.

Murchison's office was a small windowless room on the platform's upper admin level, with a one-cot examining room/sick bay immediately adjacent. Both rooms were empty as usual. The office didn't hold much—a desk, computer, and datalink setup; what Murchison didn't know how to treat already, he could look up or discuss with experts at need. He kept a small tri-vid box up on one metal shelf; he turned it to a satellite news channel and settled down to work. He listened with half an ear to the sports news—late rugby scores, mostly—as he pulled up the log page for the day on his computer screen.

0745. Wilkie, Ted, foot fungus. Treated with topical ointment, released to return to work.

The tri-vid news show cycled back to the start of the hour and the big events of the day. The main news story dealt with signs of local economic recovery after the Steel Wolves' incursion during the early summer; the show had brought in an expert from the University of New Lanark to quote statistics.

> 1156. Barton, Glynis, second-degree burn on right hand from hot oil in deep-fat fryer in galley. Applied sterile bandage, released to two days light duty.

The tri-vid news moved on to the global weather, with a story about how early snowfalls in the Rockspires presaged a hard winter, then cut to the regional weather feeds for local details. In the case of Balfour-Douglas #47, the forecast called for a high tomorrow in the southern Oilfields Coast region of 36 degrees centigrade, and an overnight low of 22.

> 1520. Calloway, Tim. Muscle aches and fever of unknown origin. Treated with acetaminophen, sent back to quarters with instructions to rest and drink plenty of water.

In the entertainment news, local Northwind networks were planning new dramas to replace off-world programming lost in the collapse of the HPG communications network: "And now an interview with producer Brett—"

The lights went out and the computer screen went blank. The office and sick bay were silent. Even the humming and ticking of the electronic equipment had suddenly ceased.

Something's happened to the power, Murchison thought.

He heard noises now: the sound of heavy feet pounding on the steel plate decks of the platform. The alarm down on Deck C began to sound—a strident, metallic pulse beat. Once it started, it could go on for hours, powered by its own stored energy, until somebody hit the manual disconnect.

Murchison kept a flashlight in his right-hand desk drawer—it had a red lens, so as not to destroy his night vision if he ever needed to use it in an emergency. He also kept a jump bag with basic medical supplies on the floor under the coatrack, to the right of the door. He checked the luminous dial of his watch. He'd wait five minutes to see if the power came back on its own, or if anyone showed up at his office with word of what was happening. Then he'd go look for himself.

He heard noises again. A high-pitched whining sound, repeated several times; the rattle of metallic impact, a long series interrupted by duller, softer bits; shouts—words, but undistinguishable—and at the end a scream.

Murchison knew that sound. Someone was in pain.

He took the flashlight out of the desk drawer, grabbed his jump bag, and headed out.

On this level, at least, no one was moving. The manager's office would be empty at this time of night anyhow—the conference room was never used except for official visitors—the security office's door was halfway open, but no one was inside. The banks of monitor screens that should have covered all the vital spaces and machinery on Balfour-Douglas #47 were off and blank.

Murchison went on downstairs to the next level, his footsteps echoing off the metal treads. He kept alert for more noises as he went, and was no longer surprised to hear, somewhere below, the sound of a slug-pistol firing a series of single shots with spaces between. He realized that he was counting, matching the number of shots against the tally of the oil rig's crew. His subconscious, at least, had already decided that something very bad was happening.

Should he stay where he was, he wondered, or go on? If matters were as bad as he feared, there was no point in cowering in his office. When they—whoever "they" were—found him, he would most likely be dead anyway. And if he was going to be dead, he might as well die doing his duty.

He opened the door to the next level, which held the berthing spaces for the oil rig's crew as well as individual quarters for staff and management. This time, the red light of his flash showed bodies, several of them.

Multiple casualties, he thought. That meant he had to do some serious triage. He was the only medic on #47, and help was hours away if it ever came at all. If he hoped to do any good, he would have to begin his work with the grim task of sorting the casualties into those who could wait for attention, those who could be helped if they were tended immediately, and those who were going to die whether they were helped immediately or not.

He had no idea what was going on, except that it was bad. All he could think of to do was what he had been trained to do, in the way he'd been trained to do it.

He took a deep breath. "Anybody who's not hurt," he called out, "come over here."

There was no response. No walking wounded, then, at least not within sound of his voice. He moved on forward, and knelt by the first body. Entrance wounds from a firearm of some sort had chewed a bloody line across the torso. He gave the man two rescue breaths. No result. He attached a black tag from the supply of them in the side pocket of his jump bag, and moved on.

The second body had half its skull fried away by what might have been a laser rifle. The body had a cooked smell, but was still breathing. A red tag, this time—marking the victim for immediate medical attention when help arrived. If help arrived. He put that thought out of his head, and moved on.

The third body lay in a spreading puddle of blood. One arm, still wearing the sterile bandage he'd put on it earlier that day, twitched feebly. He reached out to check the carotid artery for a pulse, then froze at the sound of footsteps, and looked up—past a pair of high-top boots, past shapely legs in dark trousers, up to a hand grasping a heavy slug-pistol.

The hand raised the slug-pistol and fired a single shot. The survivor Murchison had begun tending was a survivor no longer, and the medic realized that unless he was very lucky, he was himself already a dead man. He found the knowledge oddly calming. He sat back on his heels and looked all the way up.

He saw a woman dressed in tight trousers and a snug leather jacket, her long dark hair pulled tightly back. She was looking down at him and smiling, and her body and face together were seductive enough to have fulfilled all the most lurid fantasies of his younger self . . . if she hadn't just shot Glynis Barton in the head.

But she hadn't shot Ian Murchison, not yet. He took one breath, then another, the better to control his voice, and asked, "Who are you and what are you doing here?"

"I am Anastasia Kerensky," she said. "I own this platform now. And because it would be wasteful to kill a medic who has proved that he can carry out his duties even under the most trying circumstances—I also own you."

2

On most nights after dinner, the tourist-class passenger lounge on the *Monarch*-class DropShip *Pegasus* was a lively place, in spite of the fact that after the collapse of the HPG network there was no more interstellar tourism to speak of. These days, anybody traveling from one star system to another was likely to have more important reasons than mere desire for an exotic holiday, but there remained plenty of people in The Republic of the Sphere who needed to get someplace and needed do it on a budget.

The tourist-class lounge had a bar—but only one

bartender, and passengers had to fetch their own drinks rather than have subservient waitstaff shuttling back and forth. The lighting in tourist class was bright and matter-of-fact, instead of being kept atmospheric and privacy-dim. The tables, upholstery and flooring were a touch on the shabby side, their repair and replacement cycle stretched a little bit too long in favor of polishing up first class one more time.

The food in the tourist lounge, though, came out of the same galley as the food in first class. The cutlery here was stainless steel and not silver, and the napkins were plain paper rather than linen folded into the shapes of swans and starbursts, but the meals were every bit as good.

After long months spent fighting on Addicks, Captain Tara Bishop wasn't in the mood to care about silverware and fine linen. Good food served hot instead of field rations, and drinks mixed sufficiently cold and strong, were enough to keep her satisfied. The Northwind Regiments had called her home, and they wanted her there badly enough to pay for her ticket . . . but only tourist class. Northwind, after all, wasn't made of money. Captain Bishop could have paid to upgrade the ticket—she had most of her unspent back pay from Addicks burning a hole in her pocket—but she didn't care enough to bother.

Besides, first class was too quiet and well behaved. Tourist was a lot more fun. She could play poker every night until the bartender closed down the lounge to clean the tables and wash the glasses. Captain Bishop liked poker, and was good enough at it to win a respectable amount of the time. There hadn't been that much else to do on Addicks, in between clashes with the forces of Katana Tormark's Dragon's Fury—and, later, with Kev Rosse's Spirit Cats— except hone her natural talent for bluff to a keener edge.

Her meals and bed on board *Pegasus* were covered by her ticket, and she had a new post waiting for her on Northwind. She could gamble using all of her back pay and not worry if she lost. For Captain Bishop, in any case, the pleasure of the game lay in the exercise of skill. She got no gambler's buzz from the prospect of winning big or losing it all.

Two of the other three players tonight were the same as she. Captain Bishop had seen them in action for the first time last night; she'd quit the game while she was a few stones ahead, but she'd been more or less sober at the time and some of the others at the table weren't. On the other hand, the man with the eye patch and the woman with the knife up her sleeve—she probably thought it was concealed, but Captain Bishop had experience in spotting such things—had kept on nursing the same drinks all evening long.

Captain Bishop had become curious. Moved by that curiosity, she had stayed up late that night, accessing the ship's passenger records from her cabin's data console. She shouldn't have been able to do that, but life in the Northwind Regiments had taught Captain Bishop quite a number of useful skills, and computerized breaking and entering came high on the list.

The man with the eye patch and the woman with the knife—Farrell and Jones, names so bland and ordinary they had to be assumed—had come aboard separately, with paper trails pointing back to different planets. There was no reason that they should be viewed as confederates, working the crowd together. But her gut said they were, and for the same reason that she played poker herself on shipboard—sheer, complete boredom.

Captain Bishop had resolved at that moment to spend the next night having fun.

Now the players at the poker table were Bishop, the man and the woman, and the weedy-looking young gentleman whom the man and the woman appeared to be in the process of cleaning out. Bishop and the two card sharps were sober; the evening's destined victim, unsurprisingly, was not.

The victim—Thatcher Wilberforce or Wilberforce Thatcher, Captain Bishop wasn't certain which—was also running well ahead of Jones and Farrell at the moment. By design, Bishop suspected; the duo would find it amusing to let him get flushed with success, with his judgment clouded by celebratory drinks, then descend like crows on carrion.

Hah, she thought, masking her contempt with an expression of vacuous amiability. Move along, there's no dead meat for you here. I'll give you two something to think about, I will.

First, though, she had to get rid of Thatcher, or Wilberforce, or whatever his name was. Captain Bishop suppressed a pre-battle grin and set her plan into motion by turning to the young man.

"You have all the luck tonight," she told him, doing her best to sound aggrieved. "I can barely keep up, and they"—she waved a hand at Jones and Farrell in an expansive gesture—"are floundering."

Thatcher blinked. "Luck has to change sometimes. Not their turn to win, I suppose."

Captain Bishop kept her face straight with some difficulty. Lord, this one was not only drunk, but none too bright. Fleecing the likes of him should be illegal, like shooting a protected species, she thought.

"Maybe it is their turn to lose," she said. "But whose turn it is to win—that's the question."

Thatcher smiled the happy smile of the naive and stupid. "Looks like mine, doesn't it?"

Bishop put on a thoughtful expression. "Oh, I don't know." She waved a hand at her own pile of chips. "I'm not doing so bad myself tonight."

"Not so good as me."

"Exactly the point I was about to make," she said. "*Your* good luck is getting in the way of *my* good luck, and it's going to cut me out of the action when they"—she gave yet another wave, at Jones and Farrell this time—"go down."

The woman with the hidden knife looked up suddenly. "Hey, wait a—"

Bishop rounded on Jones with an air of sudden belligerence. "Hush. Thatcher and I are discussing who gets to take you to the cleaners later."

She could see Jones itching to make a quarrel of it—here was another one, she thought, who'd learned the game somewhere that wasn't well lit and well behaved—but saw her swallow the intended retort and back down. The hunt was still on, after all, and nobody wanted to startle the prey.

Bishop turned back to Thatcher and said, "The way I see it, somebody's going to take their money tonight, and it's going to be either you or me." She gave the young man a confiding, semi-tipsy smile. "I've got a proposal for you."

"What sort of proposal?" asked Thatcher. He was not yet so drunk, apparently, that he couldn't at least fake caution.

"We cut the cards," she said. "High card stays in the game, low card takes his or her money and leaves the table."

Thatcher looked dubious. "I don't think—"

No, you don't, Captain Bishop said to herself, and that's why these two are set to clean you out. Aloud, she said, "That way we don't waste our good luck on each other."

He was wavering now, she could tell. Jones and Farrell weren't looking at each other, but Captain Bishop could feel them thinking that whatever the outcome of the cut, one mark would be as good as the other. No matter who won, the duo would have their fun tonight.

Good, she thought. Keep on believing that for a little while longer.

To Thatcher she said, "I'll put fifty stones on it."

That brought a spark to the young man's eyes. "Fifty stones *and* a seat at the table?"

"You got it," she said.

"You're on."

Captain Bishop picked up the deck of cards, shuffled and squared it, then slid it over to Thatcher for his cut. He turned up the two of diamonds. She retrieved the deck, shuffled again, and made her own cut. Not feeling the need to be ostentatious, she gave herself the jack of spades.

When it came to cards, there were more kinds of skill than just one. Captain Bishop had staved off boredom, on Addicks and elsewhere, by picking up most of them.

"Sorry about that," she said to the young man—not so young, really, perhaps even slightly older than she was herself, but Lord, he made her feel ancient. "Maybe you'll get your turn another night."

Captain Bishop watched with an expression of amiable dimness as Thatcher collected his winnings and left the tourist lounge. Then she turned to Jones and Farrell with a different expression altogether.

"Well, that takes care of him," she said. She picked up the cards and began shuffling them. "And now, my friends—let's play an honest game of poker."

3

Gymnasium at the New Barracks
Tara
Northwind
November 3133; local winter

The gymnasium at the New Barracks in Tara was considerably more than its name implied. The sprawling complex, larger than many commercial arenas, existed in order to serve the physical training of all the Northwind Highlanders stationed at the fort or elsewhere in the city of Tara, in addition to providing a headquarters for the various regimental sports teams. The gymnasium's wide, domed roof covered not only the main arena but also a number of more specialized facilities—rooms with pools for swimming and diving, rooms for working out with weights and exercise machines, rooms filled with mats and bars and mirrors in which the regiment's soldiers could practice skills ranging from fencing to folk dancing.

Countess and Prefect Tara Campbell of Northwind and Paladin Ezekiel Crow currently occupied one of the smaller training rooms. The two of them were alone—the benches along the walls of the room held no spectators or fellow athletes, only the tote bags of bottled water and exercise gear that Crow and the Countess had brought with them. For propriety's sake, Tara had left the door to the room standing open.

The Countess, a petite woman with short platinum-blond hair, was wearing loose white trousers and a wraparound top secured with a black belt. The Paladin was dressed similarly, though less formally. He'd shed the quilted jacket he'd worn against the November chill, though not yet the thin leather gloves he'd worn with it. Underneath the jacket, his dark shirt and trousers, cut with enough room in them to move freely in all directions, could nevertheless have served in a pinch for everyday casual wear.

Except, Tara thought, that Crow was never casual. His plainer garments carried no explicit or implied markers for level of skill and training—which was, she suspected, exactly the point. She didn't think he was covering up a lack of proficiency, since nobody made it all the way to Paladin of the Sphere without being good at fighting both with and without weapons; so he was probably very good indeed.

Good, and devious about it as well.

Tara decided she approved. She'd used the "don't

hit me, I'm cute and harmless" act a few times herself against opponents who were stupid enough to fall for it. She smiled at Crow.

"I have to thank you for agreeing to this. I need the practice, and it's hard to find someone who can forget for a while that I'm the Prefect and the Countess—at least for long enough to give me a decent match."

"I've gone too long without exercise myself," Crow said, limbering his body by twisting it. "And for much the same reasons. So you're doing me a favor as well. What do you say . . . five minutes, first fall, or over the line?"

"Going over the line," Tara said. With a wry smile, she added, "Given the burdens of rank and command, it's the only way I'm likely to be doing it for the foreseeable future."

Crow gave her a little bow. "You know yourself, I suppose. And the line will be?"

With some difficulty, Tara kept her expression politely unrevealing. Inwardly, though, she was smiling. Crow had responded in kind to her teasing comment—meant to put him off balance—which suggested that he might, indeed, not hold back out of misplaced courtesy in the match to come.

"Make the line this row of tiles," Tara said. She pointed with her foot to the decorative border that ran around the central area of the practice room. "First one out or over—"

"Pays a forfeit of the winner's choosing," Crow said. "It's always good to have something riding on the outcome."

"Fair enough. Rules?" If they'd been trained in the

same traditions, she wouldn't have needed to ask, but that was another bit of information obscured by the Paladin's unconventional choice of practice garb.

"Nothing allowed that might be permanently damaging," Crow said, "or that might limit our ability to defend Northwind."

Tara nodded. "Seems reasonable. So . . . no eye gouging, but ear biting is allowed."

"If the Countess of Northwind desires to bite my ears, she is invited to try," Crow said. He was, Tara thought, actually smiling a little as he said it. "Shall we begin?"

Tara smiled back. "Surely."

Again Crow bowed. This time he turned the motion into a forward duck and roll that brought him to his feet close to her, but still out of her striking range.

"Nice move," she said, laughing, and spun forward with a kick intending to draw him out of line.

He didn't go for it—she would have been surprised if he had—but instead pulled off his glove and threw it at her face. She ducked, and in the moment her eyes broke contact with his, he spun forward with his own kick.

"You wore"—Tara half turned and set an arm block to trap the leg as he kicked—"those gloves on purpose, didn't you? Clever."

She had the leg, she twisted, and Crow went with the twist rather than risk a dislocation. He fell, pulled, and shot to his feet, free again and standing closer still.

"The Countess does me honor," he said, and dropped an arm around her shoulders, grasping the fabric of her thin shirt. He pulled her around, and threaded his other arm under her armpit and behind her skull, pressing her head forward. "Let's take a walk together, shall we?"

He turned her, with pressure on her head, and pushed, forcing her to walk toward the line of red tiles that marked the boundary of their fighting zone. He was pressed tight against her, front to back. The line drew closer.

Just as her foot would have had to go across, impelled by Crow's superior strength, Tara raised her free hand and clapped it over the hand that rested on the back of her neck. She pressed down hard on it, so that the Paladin couldn't have moved his hand away even if he wanted to. At the same moment, she crossed one leg in front of the other, and let herself fall forward.

She went into a clumsy roll, but Crow had to go with her—either go with her or break her neck, and break the terms of the contest at the same time. She fell, she rolled, taking both of them over the line of tiles. Then she relaxed, letting her body go limp.

"You're across the line," Crow said. The drop-and-roll had ended with him falling beneath her, and she could feel his breath stirring the hairs on the back of her neck as he spoke.

"I think," Tara said, "that you touched the ground first. Paladin."

A moment.

"Yes," Crow said. "I believe that I did."

What she would have said then in reply, Tara never knew. She heard footsteps approaching, and scrambled to her feet in time to see Brigadier General Michael Griffin pause in the practice room's open doorway. She became aware that she was more flustered than she ought to be, and equally aware of Crow—not flustered so much as suddenly hypercorrect—rising and moving to stand a few feet away, well out of personal distance.

Crow's darker coloring made his passing emotions hard to read. But for her part, Tara suspected irritably that she was blushing, and hoped that General Griffin would attribute the higher color to exertion rather than to any more inconvenient emotion. Michael Griffin and Ezekiel Crow had not worked easily together when the Paladin first came to Northwind, and Griffin had not been pleased when Crow, at Exarch Damien Redburn's request, had remained on-planet to assist with the post-war recovery. He would be even less pleased if he thought that the Countess and the Paladin were depending upon each other for more than just political support.

But General Griffin—crisply pressed and clean-shaven as always (except for the well-trimmed ginger mustache which appeared to be his one vanity)—remained the soul of politeness. "My lady. Paladin Crow."

Tara brushed a stray lock of hair out of her eyes. It was time to get it trimmed again, she thought absently. She'd kept it spiky-short ever since her teen years, but the past few months on Northwind had been so busy that she kept letting it go too long between cuts.

"What brings you here, General?" she asked, leaving unsaid the implied but clear follow-up: *And couldn't it have waited?*

But, of course, it couldn't have. General Griffin

wouldn't have interrupted one of her rare chances for private recreation without an excellent reason, and his expression showed it.

"Regimental intelligence reports, my lady," he said. "The latest DropShip to arrive in port brought disturbing news from our off-world intelligence assets, specifically from our agents-in-place on Tigress."

Tara shut her mouth on words not becoming to an already sweaty and undignified Countess. Tigress was home to the Steel Wolves, members of Clan Wolf resident in what had been—and what would remain, if Prefect Tara Campbell had any say in the matter— The Republic of the Sphere. Forces from Tigress, under the command of the Steel Wolves' new leader Anastasia Kerensky, had invaded Northwind less than a year before, only to be repulsed with hard fighting.

"What's happening on Tigress?" asked Ezekiel Crow.

"According to our agents," Griffin said, "the Steel Wolf forces that sallied from Tigress to attack Northwind have not yet returned to the Four Cities."

"Is that all?"

Griffin shook his head. "Reports also have other units departing Tigress at this time, destination unknown."

Tara, her momentary anger back under control, asked, "How fresh is this intel?"

"Not as fresh as I'd like, I'm afraid. The messenger had to make three DropShip transits—one of them in the wrong direction—before he could risk putting himself onto a ship heading home."

"Do we have any reports of Steel Wolf activity anywhere in Prefecture III after the date on this report?" Crow asked.

"Steel Wolf activity, yes," Griffin said. "But it's all small-scale stuff, and Anastasia Kerensky's name is never associated with any of the attacks."

"Could she have been challenged and lost her position?" Tara wondered. "She'd have been vulnerable, after losing to us like she did last summer."

"It's possible," said Griffin. "But a new leader would have made him- or herself known, at least on Tigress, and our agents there haven't reported any significant changes in the Wolves' command structure."

A moment of grim silence followed. Finally Tara let herself give voice to what they all had to be thinking.

"The bitch is up to something. I just know it."

4

Tourist-Class Passenger Quarters
DropShip Pegasus
en route from Addicks to Northwind
November 3133

Dianna Jones—"Dagger Di" to friends and enemies alike since the first day she'd been old enough to use a knife—was not in a good mood. The card game that had promised amusement and easy pickings had not turned out well, and Jack Farrell had added insult to injury by informing her, as they left the tourist-class lounge, that they needed to meet in his cabin for a talk. Right now she didn't feel like talking to anybody, and most especially not to One-Eyed Jack Farrell.

But personal inclinations didn't count for much

where work was concerned. And this *was* work; she certainly wasn't traveling tourist class to Northwind for pleasure, or for the sake of her health.

Grimly, she followed Jack to a cabin that, except for a trifling matter of location, turned out to be identical to her own: a small, compactly designed space that had a narrow bunk set into one bulkhead, with compartments above and below for storage. Bathing and sanitary facilities were housed in a vertical pod-like unit built into another bulkhead; passengers for whom elbow room was more important than either privacy or convenience could use the roomier lavatories down at the end of the corridor. Of the compartment's two remaining bulkheads, one was taken up by the door and the other by a combination work desk and entertainment station. The work desk was outfitted with a tri-vid, a disc player, a computer and communications console, and the room's only chair.

Dagger Di took the chair without waiting for an invitation. She pulled it away from the desk and sat straddling it, making certain as she did so to keep between Farrell and the cabin door. Maybe their boss trusted Farrell, she thought, but there was no way in hell that she was ever going to. Farrell saw what she was doing, she could tell—but only laughed, shrugged, and stretched out on the bunk.

"Get over it, darlin'. We've got work to do."

"Yeah, right." Di was irritated, and not disposed to get down immediately to business. "Who the hell was that Northwinder bitch, anyway?"

Farrell looked smug. "You should check out the passenger lists more often. She's a Captain in one of the Highlander regiments, traveling in mufti. Came aboard at Addicks, so she's seen her share of fighting lately."

"And it doesn't bother you that she walked away with all the money on the table?"

"Not particularly," said Farrell. "It's not like it was ours in the first place."

"Yes, it was," Di said. "We won it."

"And she won it back," Farrell said. "The fortunes of war, Di darling."

Di remained unmollified. "I had plans for that money. And don't call me 'darling.' "

"Make new plans, then. Unless—you weren't using mission operating funds, were you?"

"Good Lord, no!" Di shook her head vehemently. "Do I *look* that stupid?"

"No," he said, eyeing her knife hand nervously.

As well he might, she thought. After everything that had passed between the two of them, Farrell had to have more sense than to believe her stupid enough to gamble with an employer's money. Especially not when their current employer was Jacob Bannson of Bannson Universal Unlimited.

Bannson hired only the best—Dagger Di had no false modesty concerning either her own worth or Jack Farrell's—and those he hired he treated honestly. He fulfilled his part of the contract to the letter, and didn't stint on paying his employees what they were worth. But those for whom even Bannson's generous pay scale was not generous enough, who stole from him or double-crossed him, were dealt with swiftly and without mercy—and usually without bothering to involve the local law.

"I was using discretionary travel funds," Di said.

"Like you. Unless *you* decided to get stupid all of a sudden."

"Which I did not," Farrell said. "And do you see me repining over lost money? Unless I'm a worse judge of character than I think I am, we'll have our chance to win it back."

"Not with blondie keeping watch in the lounge," Di said. "We won't have a chance."

"I wouldn't go that far. She just didn't want us bankrupting poor old Thatcher."

"Wilberforce," Di corrected him.

"Whatever," Farrell said. "Under all that, the good Captain Bishop is as bored with DropShip life as we are. So long as we stay honest, she'll be glad to play."

"Honest," said Di. "Hah. She gave herself the high card. And the jack of spades is a one-eyed jack—do you think she did it to tell us that she knew who we were?"

"I think she did it because she wanted Wilberforce out of the game, and she got what she wanted."

"And you still want to play cards with her? Maybe you are stupid, after all." Di was more thoughtful now. "She's good. I hope we don't come up against her in the field."

"Anything can happen," Farrell said. "Especially in our line of work. And it never hurts to get a feel for another player's style."

5

Fort Barrett
Oilfields Coast
Northwind
November 3133; dry season

Fort Barrett was a prosperous, midsized town situated on Kearney's Oilfields Coast. The regimental post had originally served as a source of law and order for the remote district. Over the years a sizable town had sprung up around the fort, and in recent decades the entire region had grown prosperous with offshore drilling. These days Fort Barrett was a pleasant if isolated posting. The units serving there were often ones that had distinguished—and exhausted—themselves in action elsewhere, and now were being rewarded with a stint of undemanding duty in a tranquil location.

Will Elliot's scout/sniper unit was currently enjoying such a reward. During the summer, Will and his comrades had stood with Colonel—now Brigadier General—Griffin to hold the mouth of Red Ledge Pass against the Steel Wolves, buying time for Tara Campbell and Ezekiel Crow to organize the main defense, and they had fought again, without a break for rest, in the final pitched battle on the plains. They had taken heavy losses, especially for new unblooded troops, but they hadn't broken. And after the mud had dried and the Wolves had left Northwind, they had been sent to Fort Barrett to relax in the sun.

Will had been promoted to Corporal in the aftermath of the invasion, and had not found the duties of that rank to be overly burdensome. Life at Fort Barrett was, generally speaking, enjoyable, with good weather, an attractive location, and a soothing daily base routine. He wrote to his mother once a week, assuring her of his continued health and well-being, and sent half of his money to her every payday by automatic allotment.

He worried about his mother a bit sometimes. Jean Elliot was living these days in Kildare with Will's sister, Ruth, and still hadn't decided what to do about her home in Liddisdale. The house where Will and his two sisters had grown up, and where Will had continued to live with his mother until hard times had impelled him to join the Regiment, had been badly damaged in the summer's fighting. If the structure wasn't rebuilt before the end of winter, by spring it would be fit for nothing except selling it for the land beneath it.

This being late afternoon on a mail day, Will had just sent his mother another letter, in handwritten hardcopy since she didn't like using her daughter's communications console. (She fretted that Ruth might begrudge her the connection time, although Ruth had assured Will privately more than once that she did nothing of the kind.) Will had also picked up a soft but bulky package from Kildare which he suspected contained hand-knitted woolen socks—his mother made them for him every winter. He wasn't likely to need them here on the coast, but if he'd figured out one thing about life in the Regiment, it was that you never knew where you might be going next.

He left the post office with the package of socks tucked under one arm, and stepped out into the brilliant sunlight of the parade ground. The sky overhead was a bright eye-watering blue, and a stiff breeze had the banners of Northwind and the Regiment and The Republic of the Sphere snapping on their flagpoles. The air smelled of salt water and warm-climate flowers, with a faint underlying note of distant oil refinery. In the carefully tended flower beds beneath the post office windows, myriad insects buzzed and whirred.

He was halfway across the parade ground, and the sun dazzle had not quite cleared from his vision, when he crossed the path of Master Sergeant Murray—a short, muscular man who possessed the seemingly miraculous ability to keep his uniform in fresh-pressed condition on the muddiest of battlefields.

"Elliot," Murray said.

Will halted. "Sergeant."

"I've been looking for you."

Being looked for by a sergeant was never good. Will searched his conscience hastily for possible errors and infractions, and came up clean. He suppressed the urge to panic anyway and said, "Sergeant?" in tones of respectful inquiry.

"The company has a problem, Elliot. With Foster going down to Halidon to train with the battle-armor boys, we're short a sergeant. That means we're going to have to promote somebody, and the Captain says that it ought to be you."

"Me, Sergeant?" Will felt blank and startled. The promotion to corporal hadn't particularly surprised him. He'd known he was good enough at the job for that, and besides, they'd lost enough men at Red Ledge Pass and on the plains that they would have had to promote somebody regardless. But he hadn't thought that things were still so bad they'd need to promote him again.

"You want to tell Captain Fletcher that he doesn't know what he's doing?" Murray asked.

"No. But—" Will paused. He'd had an unpleasant thought. "Sergeant, is there trouble coming that nobody's talking about?"

Murray gave him an approving look. "No trouble right now—but you know how to think about things, Elliot. That's good. Be at the admin building at 1000 tomorrow to sign the papers."

They parted, and Will, feeling a bit light-headed, continued back to the shadowy coolness of the barracks. There, he found his friends Jock Gordon and

Lexa McIntosh—the former a muscular giant of a
man and the latter a diminutive gypsy-dark
woman—passing the time quietly at the end of their
duty day.

Jock was a farm boy from New Lanark, the youngest of too many brothers, and Lexa had run wild
with the youth gangs of the Kearney outback until a
judge—perhaps seeing a bit of potential that she herself had not—had given her a choice between time
in the Regiment and time in jail. At the moment Jock
was polishing the already gleaming buttons and
buckles of his dress uniform, and Lexa was lying on
her stomach in her bunk reading a six-month-old
copy of *FashionSphere*.

She looked up from the magazine's pages as Will
approached. "Hey, Will. It says here that open-toed
pumps are coming back into style. Do you think I
should buy myself some the next time we get paid?"

"Go for it," Jock said, when Will didn't answer.
"They'll be just the thing for those long marches."

"Once in a while I do go somewhere that doesn't
involve hiking twenty-five miles and shooting people
at the end of it," Lexa replied. She trailed off, looking
at Will, who hadn't said anything. "Will? Are you
all right?"

He sat down heavily on his bunk, still clutching
the package from his mother. "Um," he said. "Yes.
I'm all right—I'm fine. Really."

"Well, you look like somebody hit you over the
head with a sock full of sand. Not that I'd know
about that from experience, mind you."

Jock set aside his rag and his can of polish and

gave Will his full attention. "Is it bad news from home?"

"No." The word came out sounding fainter than Will intended. He tried again, and this time achieved a normal voice. "It's—Master Sergeant Murray says they're going to promote me. To Sergeant."

Lexa turned to Jock. "Told you they'd do it before New Year's. Pay up."

Will looked from one of his friends to the other. "Did everybody see this coming except me?"

Jock grinned. "Aye."

"What am I going to do?" Will asked plaintively.

"Your job, what else?" said Lexa. "In the meantime, since it's payday and they haven't actually pinned the stripes on you yet—let's all go out tonight and celebrate while you're still poor and humble enough to socialize with the likes of us."

6

Prefect's Office
New Barracks
Tara
Northwind
November 3133; local winter

For the first time in several years, Captain Tara Bishop was back in the city with which she (like the Countess of Northwind) shared a name. A great deal had happened during the time she had been gone, and a lot of things had changed. She'd been nothing more than a green Lieutenant Junior Grade when she left home to join the Highlander forces serving offworld—and The Republic of the Sphere had been a happy and peaceful place, with the HPG communications network up and running, providing the thread of regular, almost real-time contact that tied together The Republic's scattered political entities.

The Lieutenant Tara Bishop of those days had not anticipated seeing any combat harder than the occasional skirmish with pirates or with disaffected political extremists. Fighting against the latter, especially, seemed almost unfair, since as a class they tended to be chronically underfunded and undersupported, the last political resort of perpetual losers and hopeless romantics.

That was then, Captain Bishop reminded herself as she made her way through the streets of the capital. This is now.

And "now" meant a universe in which the HPG net had gone down, at the hands of one or another of a dozen different parties, all claiming responsibility for the job, although Captain Bishop remained more than half convinced that the real culprit was somebody else who wasn't talking about the job at all. In that new universe, every fringe group and neo-factionalist in the Inner Sphere was suddenly raising an army and trying to carve out an area of influence. Case in point, the Dragon's Fury on Addicks—and while Captain Bishop had been fighting there, keeping the Kurita Dragon's grasping claws away from a peaceful world with no real standing army to put up a defense, her own home planet had come under attack.

To her unspoken but profound relief, Northwind's capital city and its main DropPort showed few obvious marks of the fighting. She knew from the reports she'd read en route from Addicks that the final battle had taken place away from built-up areas, in the open farm and grazing land of the plains north of Tara; she'd seen pictures, and knew that in a season or two most of the scars of combat would be gone.

On the other hand, the homes and small towns along the road through Red Ledge Pass had not been so fortunate. Captain Bishop had gone skiing and rock climbing in that area, and the place-names attached to stories of the Steel Wolves' trail of destruction were ones she remembered from holidays past: Harlaugh, Liddisdale, the Killie Burn, all of them wrecked or polluted, and needing far longer than a couple of seasons to repair.

The changes in the capital, once she started looking for them, proved to be more subtle. Soldiers in uniform were a more common sight than they'd been in the days before the HPG collapse, a reminder that the Highlander Regiments were expanding in size for the first time in some decades. Prices these days were higher than Captain Bishop remembered, driven upward by war and uncertainty. She was glad that she'd kept—and augmented by some judicious participation in games of skill—her pay from Addicks, and equally glad that she could count on finding meals and a bed waiting for her at the New Barracks.

First things first, though. Before she could settle in to her new quarters, she had to present herself and her orders to Prefect Tara Campbell. She'd taken the time before leaving the DropShip to freshen up, putting on a clean uniform and a touch of cosmetics— not enough to look gaudy, just enough to show that she took the occasion seriously enough to make an effort—and had brushed some order back into her short blond hair.

At least it's my natural color, she reflected. I know for a fact that the Countess dyes hers.

This irreverent thought cheered her as she passed through the front gate of the fort complex with a flip of an ID card, and made her way to the New Barracks and another ID check, and then at last to Tara Campbell's offices. The Countess was in. Like everything else on Northwind, Tara Campbell had changed since the last time Captain Bishop had seen her. She looked older than she had when Captain Bishop met her on Addicks, and tireder as well, as though she'd been getting by for too long on too few hours of sleep a night.

She looked harder, too, in a way that Captain Bishop couldn't quite put a finger on, except to say that she looked like someone who'd made the tough decisions.

Captain Bishop saluted and handed across her orders.

"Captain Tara Bishop reporting for duty as ordered, ma'am."

"At ease, Captain, and take a seat." The Prefect waited, smiling politely—she had grown up around diplomats, and would probably smile politely even if you set her hair on fire—while Captain Bishop complied. Then she continued, "I see that you're going to be my new aide."

"Yes, ma'am," Captain Bishop said.

"Excellent." The Prefect smiled again, and this time it looked genuine. "I've been making do with temporarily assigned personnel ever since the battle on the plains, and it hasn't been working out as well as I'd like. Having someone who's actually up to handling the responsibilities of the job may let me get some rest."

"I hope to do a good job, ma'am," Captain Bishop said.

"Of course you do. Your Colonel speaks highly of you; he wouldn't have recommended you for the post if he didn't think you were capable."

"Yes, ma'am." Captain Bishop also remembered her Colonel telling her—when she complained to him about having to leave Addicks—that a post as aide to the Prefect was a big step upward in the direction of better things, and one that most career minded young officers would be damned grateful to get. He'd also said that the Countess of Northwind wasn't merely a political soldier. She wouldn't hang back when fighting needed to be done, and anyone serving as her aide would see all the action that she ever wanted.

"The very first thing we have to get clear," Tara Campbell said, "is that if you're going to be any good to me as an aide, you're going to have to speak freely, like you did back on Addicks. None of this 'yes ma'am' and 'no ma'am' stuff. Tell the truth and shame the devil, as my father used to say."

"Yes, ma'—" Captain Bishop caught herself. "I'll do my best. But it's a lot easier out in the field."

The Countess of Northwind laughed. "Believe me, Captain Bishop, you're not the first person ever to notice that."

═══ 7 ═══

Riggers' Rest Inn
Fort Barrett
Oilfields Coast
Northwind
November 3133; dry season

When Anastasia Kerensky had returned to Northwind, the last place she'd expected to find herself spending an evening—spending several evenings, in fact—was drinking beer incognito in a Fort Barrett pub, even with her trusted officer and occasional lover Nicholas Darwin along for escort and backup. Disguise and subterfuge did not suit her temperament. While she was fighting for The Republic on Dieron and Achernar as Tassa Kay, she had reveled in the high-visibility accomplishments of her other self, and never bothered to change either her looks or her manners. Tassa Kay had simply been a version of Anastasia Kerensky cut loose from the bonds of Clan and Bloodname, free instead to act as she pleased in all things. She had enjoyed being Tassa Kay.

This time, though, she had been forced to adopt an identity so far from her own that it chafed like an ill-fitting shoe. She had temporarily lightened her long hair from its distinctive lustrous black with reddish highlights to a plain drab brown—she would be glad when she could reverse the effect, but for now it was necessary for her to appear the opposite of flamboyant. She had traded her snug black leather jacket and trousers for practical traveler's gear: sturdy thick-soled shoes and bulky socks; hiking shorts and a loose shirt and a floppy wide-brimmed hat; a backpack and a walking stick.

Her entire outfit came from the crew lockers on the captured offshore oil rig. The medic, Ian Murchison, had found the items for her at her instruction, and the hair-color kit as well, though with an expression that said he had not enjoyed the task. All things considered, however, the oil rig's sole surviving crew member was adjusting to his Bondsman status as much as anyone was likely to who wasn't already Clan.

Nicholas Darwin was similarly outfitted, and from the same source, although in Anastasia's opinion the outdoor-tourist look worked considerably better on him than it did on her. He was a compactly built man, not overlarge but quite strong, as befitted a Warrior who fought his battles from the cramped interior of a tank, and the hiking shorts showed off his dark skin and his well-muscled legs to excellent advantage.

Anastasia and Nicholas had been waiting at the Riggers' Rest for over a week now, in the guise of travelers on a hiking tour of the Oilfields Coast. They had worked up a cover story to explain their unfamiliar accents, but Fort Barrett's booming oil economy had drawn in so many offworlders over the past couple of decades that they never needed to use it.

They had been brought to Fort Barrett by a mysterious coded message that had come in over the main communications rig in Balfour-Douglas #47. Such a message should never have made it through to Anastasia Kerensky at all. The Steel Wolves had communications and intelligence specialists hard at work making certain that the drilling station's customary flow of messages and reports never faltered. So far as the outside world knew, Balfour-Douglas #47 was still operating normally.

Nevertheless, a message had come through, and from a source who should never have known where she was, let alone how to contact her: *Fort Barrett. You pick the place. I'll find you there. We want to talk business.*

That message had led directly to twelve days spent drinking local beer out of heavy glass mugs and eating dried salted jellyfish skins. The jellyfish skins were a popular local bar food, of the sort that visiting offworlders were expected to try once and write home about shuddering; by now Anastasia was half worried she was starting to develop a taste for them.

"I do not like this," she said.

"You could have fooled me," Nicholas Darwin said. "That makes the second bowl of those things that you have finished this evening."

"Not the food," she said. "This waiting for a person who does not give their name."

"You said you knew who it came from."

Anastasia took a long drink from her mug of beer. She wished that it were vodka, but the Riggers' Rest was not the sort of place to have the good stuff in stock. Besides, vodka was the drink of choice for her alter ego Tassa Kay in a hell-raising mood, and she was not being Tassa Kay now. She was merely Anastasia in disguise.

"We both know who it had to come from," she said. "But he is not going to come to us himself. So we wait, looking like fools, for someone whom we will not know when we meet."

Thinking of it, she had to suppress the urge to twist her face into a snarl. Mousy brown backpackers did not do that sort of thing. She would wait, she would listen to the envoy from that person who believed that he had business with the Steel Wolves. And someday, when matters on Northwind had been settled for good and all, Anastasia Kerensky would show that person exactly what it meant to do business with Clan Wolf.

But not now, it seemed. The barmaid had just brought over a fresh mug of beer to Nicholas Darwin, along with a small folded slip of paper.

"From the lady over there," the barmaid said.

Anastasia looked without turning her head, and saw a young red-haired woman dressed in stylish but practical clothes—if by "practical" one meant

"conveniently tailored for concealed weapons."
Nicholas Darwin unfolded the note, read it, and
passed it over to Anastasia without a word.

> The lady needs to meet with me alone. Room
> 9, upstairs, in ten minutes.

"You should not go alone," Darwin said after she
had finished reading the message. "It might be a
trap."

"If I do not go alone, she will vanish for the night
and we will have to do this all over again. And I am
tired of drinking beer in Fort Barrett."

"Good point," he conceded. "Even beer gets boring after a while. What should I do, then?"

"Wait downstairs and listen. If you hear me call
out to you by name, come running with your weapons ready in your hands."

Darwin nodded. "I can do that."

"Good."

Ten minutes passed. The other woman had left the
room as soon as her note was delivered. Other parties
came and went, off-shift refinery workers leaving the
Riggers' Rest as soldiers from Fort Barrett proper came
in. Anastasia rose and drained the last of her beer.

"It is time. Wait for me here, and remember—
listen."

She went up the narrow stairs to the inn's second
floor, and down the hallway to room 9, at the far end.
The door was not latched, and stood slightly ajar.

Anastasia pushed on the door a little. It opened. She
stepped inside, and the door swung shut. Hearing no
sound of an automatic lock clicking over, she

suppressed—for the moment—the urge to react violently, and looked around the room for the other woman.

She found her sitting by the writing desk in the corner opposite the door.

"Hello, Galaxy Commander," the woman said. "I see that you got our message."

Anastasia took the room's other chair without waiting for an invitation. "First things first. Who are you, and how were you able to get that message through?"

"Don't worry about me," the woman said. "I'm just the hired help. As for how my principal was able to get a message through to you—I'm afraid that's proprietary information."

"Whose information? And whose hired help?"

"I think you know."

"I know whose name was mentioned," Anastasia said. "But anyone can mention a name."

The woman smiled. "Maybe so. But Jacob Bannson isn't a name it pays to mention if you don't have the man himself backing you up. Which, as it happens, I do."

"Explain to me why I should believe you."

"I thought I might have to do that," the woman said. "So I asked the boss for this."

She pulled a disc out of the pocket of her tailored jacket and inserted it into the room's battered tri-vid player. The display unit filled with staticky fuzz which cleared in a few seconds to show an image of Bannson himself. The strong facial features and the full red-orange beard were unmistakable, like a viking of old in a well-cut suit; not for the first time, Anastasia suspected that he cultivated the look on purpose.

Bannson spoke. "The bearer of this disc is acting in accordance with my wishes and is empowered to enter into negotiations in my name. Her likeness is presented now for your comparison."

The face in the tri-vid changed to an image of the other woman. Anastasia studied it, and was forced to concede that it was a match.

"So you really are who you say you are." She reached out and turned the tri-vid off. "What does your employer want from me?"

"*From* you?" the woman asked. "Nothing. In fact, my employer wants to help you achieve your goals."

"How?"

"By offering you the assistance of a unit or more of trusted mercenaries, including artillery, battle armor, and 'Mechs."

Anastasia stiffened. "Please convey my thanks to your employer, and let him know that my Wolves and I do not desire mercenary assistance at the present time."

"Is that your last word on the subject?"

"It is my only word."

The other woman shrugged. "Whatever you say. But the offer remains open." She took the disc out of the player and slipped it back into her pocket. Then she gave Anastasia a level look. "And a word of advice from me to you, purely out of the kindness of my heart—"

Anastasia was still offended. "Yes?"

"Clean up your own house before somebody outside cleans it for you. How do you think we got your secret frequency?"

8

Riggers' Rest Inn
Fort Barrett
Oilfields Coast
Northwind
November 3133; dry season

Will, Jock, and Lexa were celebrating Will's imminent promotion at the Riggers' Rest. The inn was not so fancy a dining place that the management would throw out a trio of foot soldiers for daring to drink in the bar. "If our uniforms aren't good enough to pass the dress code," Lexa had decreed when they started out for the evening, "then we don't want to go there."

On the other hand, it was close enough to uptown to serve good food as well as good booze, and the owner had a soft spot for the men and women of the Regiments, being a discharged twenty-year veteran who'd bought the inn with his mustering out pay. It was, in short, an ideal spot in which to celebrate a promotion.

The time was the odd midway hour of the day, a bit too late to count as afternoon, a bit too early to be called evening, and the bar of the Riggers' Rest was mostly deserted. What looked like the local after work crowd was filtering out as Will and his two friends entered, and the dinner crowd had not yet shown up.

Jock and Lexa were already intent on getting drunk—or if not completely drunk, at the very least well-lubricated. Will was amused; this was his party, but it looked like he'd gotten stuck with being the sober one again tonight.

The same thing had happened at the victory party in the White Horse back in Tara, after the battle on the plains. He supposed it was a reflex left over from his civilian days, when he'd worked as a wilderness guide leading parties of off-world tourists through the forests of the Rockspire Mountains. Put him in the company of people determined to be foolish, and he felt responsible for making certain they all got home.

If life as a soldier hadn't kicked that impulse out of him, he supposed that nothing ever would. There would be no hell-raising for Sergeant-to-be Will Elliot tonight. He resigned himself to nursing his original mug of beer and enjoying a grilled seafood platter instead.

"Try the jellyfish skins," Lexa said, halfway through the spread of appetizers.

Will looked at the bowl full of salt-encrusted, semi-transparent flakes. "The what?"

Lexa gave him a wicked grin. "Jellyfish skins. The coast here is the only place you can get them made fresh. Flash-irradiated isn't the same."

"I don't know—"

"Trust your auntie Lexa. It's probably the last chance you'll get."

An awkward silence fell over the table. Lexa had stated a truth they had been avoiding. After tonight, the three of them would never have quite the same easy friendship as before. The difference in rank, however slight, would always be there, coloring their interactions with obligations and duties on Will's part that the other two did not share.

He found himself hoping that promotion would come their way as well, to ease the unwanted estrangement, but could not help feeling dubious. Jock Gordon was steady as granite, but not a particularly fast or imaginative thinker; Lexa McIntosh was fast and imaginative, all right—and a crack shot with any weapon that needed aiming—but she hadn't completely lost the wild streak that had landed her in the Regiment to start with.

Will drew back from that line of thought with an inward sigh. He wasn't accustomed to thinking of his friends in that manner—it had been somebody else's job to do so until now. Feeling vaguely guilty, he scooped up a handful of the jellyfish skins and crunched them down. They tasted surprisingly good.

"I give up," he told Lexa. "You were right."

"Of course I'm right. Your turn, Jock—you try them."

Jock shook his head doubtfully. He was never an eager candidate for new experiences. "I don't know. . . ."

"Do you want everyone to think that you're a tourist?" Lexa demanded.

"I am a tourist."

"You're not a tourist," Will told him. "You're a soldier stationed here, which is a different thing altogether." Will looked about the bar, scanning the handful of patrons, and found what he was looking for. "*That* is a tourist."

Jock and Lexa glanced in the direction he'd indicated. A young man sat alone at a table drinking beer, dressed for hiking with a backpack propped against the wall beside him. He hadn't come to the Riggers' Rest alone; another backpack and a walking stick stood next to his.

"How do you know he's a tourist?" Lexa asked.

Jock nodded agreement. "Lots of people hike."

"He's a tourist," Will said definitely. "I used to work with them; I can tell." He continued, warming to his topic. "That guy isn't from anywhere around here."

"Want to bet on it?" asked Lexa.

"Sure." Will wasn't a gambler; but this wasn't a gamble, any more than betting that snow would close Breakbone Pass sometime during the winter. "Five stones says he isn't from Kearney at all."

Lexa said, "We'll take it."

"Where are we going to get the answer?" Jock asked.

"From him." Will looked at Lexa. "Do you want to ask him, or shall I?"

"Better be you," Lexa said. "He had a girl with him earlier, and she'll be coming back any minute."

"You sure?"

"You know what you know and I know what I know. He doesn't look like a guy who's just been dumped and abandoned."

Will got up and went to the other table. He thought about the problem briefly on his way over, and decided that the direct approach was the best. There was no point in concocting an elaborate excuse when a simple request for information would work just as well.

"I'm sorry to bother you," he said politely to the young man, "but I wonder if you'd mind helping my friends and me settle an argument."

The man looked doubtful, but also curious. "An argument?"

"Well, actually," Will said sheepishly, "we have a bet going."

The man glanced from Will over to Jock and Lexa. "A bet, you say?"

"Aye."

"And how am I supposed to be able to help you with it?"

"Tell us where you're from, and if I've guessed the right answer I win five stones from each of them."

The man looked amused. "I have heard stupider bets in my time, and made a few. Here—I will write it on the napkin, so they will not say you cheated."

He scrawled something on the napkin with a pen from his shirt pocket. Will took the napkin without looking at it.

"Thanks," he said.

He returned to his friends and handed the napkin to Lexa. "Well? What does it say?"

"I'm impressed—" she began.

"It says he's impressed?"

"No, you jumped-up rock climber, it says he's from Thorin."

"The planet?" Jock said.

Lexa nodded. "Unless there's a town with the same name somewhere in Prefecture X, which he also says he's from. Looks like we pay up, Jocko."

Will took their money and put it away, frowning distractedly as he did so. Lexa raised an eyebrow at him.

"Something wrong?"

"Thorin's a long way from here."

"Like you said, he's a tourist."

"I know," Will said. "I met a few tourists from Thorin, back when I was working as a mountain guide. He doesn't sound like he's from Thorin."

"Maybe he was born somewhere else," Jock said. "People move around, you know."

Will thought of his mother, looking more and more like she would be settling permanently with his sister in Kildare, while the house in Liddisdale turned into rubble from lying untended. "I know. It's just—"

"Hey," said Lexa. "Told you his girl would come back."

The woman who came down from the upper part of the inn and joined the man from Thorin was also, by her dress, a tourist. But the man's expression as she joined him prompted Will to give her a second look, and to see that the dull brown hair in its practical style framed a striking, strong-boned face, and

that the hiking shorts and loose shirt failed dismally
to hide an equally striking body.

"Quit drooling, Will," Lexa told him. "She's
taken."

"It's not that."

"What is it then, if it isn't that?"

Will shook his head. "It's . . . something. I don't
know. Probably nothing."

He put the nagging uncertainty aside, and applied
himself to his dinner. It was not until several hours
later, back in his bunk at the fort, that the question
and its answer came to him in a flash of memory,
overlaying the face he'd seen at the Riggers' Rest
with another face, one that he'd seen over and over
again in the tri-vid news during the aftermath of last
summer's war.

The leader of the Steel Wolves.

Anastasia Kerensky.

=== 9 ===

The motor whaleboat belonging to Balfour-Douglas #47 cut through the waves with Nicholas Darwin at the tiller, bearing Galaxy Commander Anastasia Kerensky home from the Oilfields Coast. Anastasia was not certain why the 26-foot open craft should have been called a whaleboat, since to the best of her knowledge Northwind had no indigenous aquatic mammals, and even on Terra itself nobody had hunted whales for centuries. She'd asked Ian Murchison about the name, thinking that as a former member of the oil rig's crew he might know the reason, but the Bondsman had only shrugged and said, "It's a sailor thing."

"There are no sails on this—whaleboat—either," she had said.

"Don't ask me, Galaxy Commander. I'm just the medic."

Anastasia would be happier, she thought, when the Steel Wolves were back on land. Land, air, or space—those, she knew, and land especially, where the BattleMechs ruled. She wanted to be striding across open ground in her custom-modified *Ryoken II*, dealing out carnage and destruction. All this bouncing around on choppy ocean water in a small open boat was not to her taste, even if it had been necessary in order to rendezvous with Jacob Bannson's envoy.

"I do not like it." She had been silent for some time; now she began talking again, in an attempt to distract herself from the up-and-down movement of the motor whaleboat. It was a long boat ride out to the oil rig, and #47 was not yet visible on the western horizon.

Nicholas Darwin, damn him, was not affected by the whaleboat's motion. He even knew how to steer the thing, which caused Anastasia to wonder what he had done with himself on Tigress before throwing his lot in with the Steel Wolves. He was a half-breed, freeborn to a local woman; he had come to Clan Wolf out of choice. Now he glanced at Anastasia sidelong and said, "Do not like what?"

"Bannson," she said. "Offering me gifts out of the blue."

Darwin looked amused. "Courtship by proxy? They do say he wants to found a new Great House."

"Whatever he wants from me, it is not that," she stated definitely. "He has never met me, and will not have heard of me before I challenged Kal Radick."

Though he might, she thought, have heard of Tassa Kay. Anastasia had not bothered to keep a low profile when she was traveling—and fighting for The Republic of the Sphere—as Tassa, and if Bannson proved either clever enough or well-informed enough to link the two names based on intelligence reports alone, he was even more dangerous than she had thought.

"Jacob Bannson is playing a chess game for power in The Republic of the Sphere," she said, "and he wants me to be one of his pieces. But it is not going to work."

"No?" asked Darwin.

"I will not be a pawn in anybody else's game. Not while I have the ability to be a queen in my own."

"Bannson is not someone it pays to have for an enemy."

"He does his fighting with money," Anastasia said.

"He is 'Mech qualified. That takes more than money." Darwin sounded thoughtful. The floppy cloth brim of his borrowed tourist-hiker's hat overshadowed his eyes, making it difficult for Anastasia to judge his expression.

The whaleboat was bouncing about harder now; the wind had picked up some, and the waves had curls of white on their tops. Anastasia swallowed and kept talking. "You certainly sound impressed by him." Her voice came out sharper than she had intended.

"No," said Darwin. "But I do not wish to see you underestimating him." He paused and looked away. This time she thought he might deliberately be using the shadow of his hat brim to hide the emotion on his face. "The way that Kal Radick underestimated you."

That was direct enough as warnings went, Anastasia thought. Kal Radick was dead. She had killed the former Galaxy Commander and leader of the Steel Wolves with her bare hands in a Trial of Possession, and had taken his rank and the Wolves both. She had been able to do so in large part because Radick had not seen her as dangerous until moments before the end.

"Tell me about Bannson, then," she said.

Jacob Bannson's business activities in The Republic of the Sphere had never affected distant Arc Royal, and Anastasia had heard of him only in the vaguest of general terms. If the tycoon had decided to mix himself in the Steel Wolves' affairs, however, she definitely needed to learn more. Such a talk would have the added advantage of distracting her from the threat of motion sickness brought on by the whale-boat's erratic motion through the choppy water. Ian Murchison had suggested that she prepare herself with a medication taken in advance; she had waved the idea aside on the grounds that a person who was qualified to ride a 'Mech would not be susceptible. She thought now that she should have listened to the medic in the first place.

"Bannson," said Nicholas Darwin in a thoughtful tone. He looked away for a moment, out toward the western horizon, where Balfour-Douglas #47 was now visible as a distant gray blur. Oceangoing scavenger birds wheeled in the air above it, small black dots against the blue. "Do you want the stuff that gets broadcast about him on the tri-vids, or the stories that get told about him on the streets?"

"Both."

"All right. The short official version first. He was born on St. Andre—the family was not in rags, but they were not citizens either. They had a small business."

"What kind?"

He shrugged. "Selling something, I think. Jacob Bannson left his school without graduating—this is an important thing on some worlds in The Republic because without graduation papers it is hard to find employment—in order to work for his parents. The business had some kind of trouble, but Bannson turned it around inside a year, and ended up owning all his competition while he was at it. After that, he kept on going."

So far, Anastasia thought, she was hearing only the biography of a shopkeeper, writ large. There was nothing about this story that could explain a man who cultivated the image of a raider of old; nothing that could account for the weight she had already learned was given to his name. "What does the street gossip say?"

"That the competition Bannson took over was the same one who had almost forced his parents' business into bankruptcy. And that he did not just take over the man's company, he ruined him outright—left him stripped too naked to start over."

"A man who doesn't believe in sparing his enemies, then." Anastasia Kerensky felt inclined to approve. "Go on."

"He had made enemies," Darwin said, "growing so wealthy so fast. They accused him of something— of breaking The Republic's rules for how business ought to be conducted, I am not sure how. All anybody knows is that inside three years all of his accusers were found guilty of even worse crimes than mere rule breaking, and that Bannson supplied the evidence. After that, nobody dared to cross him. It took The Republic of the Sphere itself to stop him from expanding his financial empire into Prefecture III."

"He lost very little time making up for it once the HPG net went down," Anastasia said. The whaleboat was approaching the oil rig now. Nicholas Darwin steered the craft deftly between the platform's giant metal legs and into the calmer, shadowed waters beneath. Anastasia drew a deep breath and released it. Then she asked, "Do you think he could have done it himself? Brought the net down on purpose to take advantage of the disruption?"

"Nobody knows," said Darwin. "And nobody wants to ask."

10

Captain Tara Bishop had to admit that her new post as aide-de-camp to the Countess of Northwind had its benefits—the present opportunity to spend a long working weekend as a guest in the Countess's family castle being one of them. Castle Northwind was a large gray stone structure, unabashedly pseudomedieval in design; the Countess had described it earlier to Captain Bishop as looking like the combined good-parts version of Edinburgh Castle, Carnarvon, and the Tower of London, with all the modern amenities built in.

Today the Countess was in residence, along with
Paladin Ezekiel Crow. Their personal banners flew
from the castle's parapets along with the banners of
Northwind and of the Regiments. And where the
Countess was, there her aide was also. The three of
them were at work in the castle's lesser hall, a large
rectangular room with a vaulted timber ceiling. Comfortable upholstered chairs and a long worktable of
polished dark wood had been set up in front of the
big granite hearth, and a wood fire blazed in the
massive cast-iron grate.

Off to one side another table, also of dark wood,
supported a row of silver warming dishes with
domed lids. The warming dishes held a selection of
breakfast delicacies brought up from the kitchen by
the castle's resident staff, all of whom seemed genu-
inely happy to have the Countess and her aide and
a Paladin of The Sphere in temporary residence. Captain Bishop supposed that with the Countess living
in the New Barracks, or even off world, for most of
the year, the lives of the castle staff lacked interest a
great deal of the time. They would be pleased at the
chance to show off their expertise to strangers.

Captain Bishop was pleased as well. She was not
so long away from Addicks that she failed to appreciate a post that came with the choice of kippered sil-
verlings or baked eggs in saffron sauce for a casual
working breakfast, not to mention the choice between
a bottomless pot of finest imported Capellan black
tea and an equally bottomless urn of Terran dark
roast coffee.

At the moment she was working on her first mug
of coffee—the Paladin and the Countess didn't share

her taste for the beverage, preferring the more tradi-
tional tea—and listening to a discussion of the problems inherent in a postwar economic recovery. This
weekend was dedicated to administrative work, and
specifically to the ongoing cleanup process after the
past summer's military campaign.

Routing the Steel Wolves had not left the Countess
and the Paladin without employment. Northwind
had problems enough to keep any number of people
busy. The Bloodstone region in particular was suffer-
ing from economic depression because the fighting
in Red Ledge Pass had resulted in extensive damage
to the local infrastructure.

"We've got the road repairs done, at least," Tara
Campbell said. "That was a priority. Highway 66 at
Red Ledge is the single year-round road through the
northern Rockspires."

"You know the local situation better than I," said
Crow, with the air of one conceding a point.

Captain Bishop got the impression that this was
merely the latest round in a discussion between Tara
Campbell and Ezekiel Crow that had been going on
for long time before she arrived. She was finding the
relationship between the Countess and the Paladin
interesting to watch. The two of them seemed hyper-
conscious of each other, each one watching covertly
while the other was looking away, then quickly
glancing elsewhere as soon as their eyes met.

That not-quite exchange of glances, and the way
that Tara Campbell and Ezekiel Crow unconsciously
maneuvered around the worktable—so that they always wound up a fraction inside formal speaking
distance, but never quite close enough for actual

touching—were enough to convince Captain Bishop that the two of them shared a powerful attraction. Bishop wondered if they'd figured the attraction out for themselves yet. If a specimen like Crow had been giving *her* looks like that, she'd have made a point of looking back by now.

Crow was still talking. "But you can't neglect military preparedness." He picked up a folder of printouts from the table and gestured with it. "We've got recommendations here from senior regimental staff, in favor of continuing the buildup, and their arguments are most persuasive."

Tara Campbell gave an audible sigh. "The Prefect of Prefecture III agrees with you wholeheartedly, Paladin Crow. But the Countess of Northwind has a voice in this argument too, and she's reminding the Prefect that unemployment in the Bloodstone region is up to 19 percent, that our main DropPort is only functioning at three-quarters capacity, and that the planetary economy hasn't yet fully recovered from the destabilizing effects of the HPG crash. We have to take more than the military situation into account when we're portioning out resources which are, unfortunately, finite."

"The negative consequences—" Crow began.

"Are considerable, no matter which way we fall into error. So we'll keep on robbing Peter to pay Paul, and borrowing from Paul to compensate Peter for his losses, and cutting nonessentials wherever we can." The Countess of Northwind sighed again. "Not that any two people on Northwind have ever managed to agree on what's essential and what's not."

Crow nodded. "If we hold social services funding at current levels—"

"It'll mean writing off the mountain communities," protested Tara Campbell. "They don't have enough private money to take up the slack." She paused, thinking. "Kearney's booming, though; we could divert resources from there. They'll bitch and moan, but so long as all they do is bitch and moan . . . let's have a look at those spreadsheets again."

The Countess and the Paladin went back to going over the spreadsheet printouts together, their heads closer than ever, talking to one another in low voices. Captain Bishop left them to it. She refilled her coffee mug from the big silver urn with the Northwind crest, and returned to her own job of dealing with the Prefect's incoming message traffic.

Some of the traffic was stuff that had no business being brought to the Prefect's attention at all. There was a surprising amount of that, and all of it got sent back with a stern note about making sure that it reached the proper recipient. Another, smaller portion of the traffic could be handled routinely by the Prefect's aide without the Prefect needing anything besides a summary after the fact. There was quite a bit of that stuff as well, and dealing with it constituted the main part of Captain Bishop's day-to-day job. Slightly rarer were problems for which the Prefect's aide could recommend a course of action, and for which she could expect—on most occasions—to have her recommendations followed.

Finally, there were those very rare messages which had to be brought to the Prefect's personal attention immediately, if not sooner. Captain Tara Bishop hadn't really been expecting to encounter an example of the last kind of problem, but life in the Regiment had a way of presenting people with the unexpected. Five minutes into dealing with the morning traffic, she laid a message printout onto the big table next to the stack of heavily annotated spreadsheets.

The Countess of Northwind picked up the message and read it, then passed on the sheet of paper to Ezekiel Crow.

"This changes everything," she said to the Paladin. "If Anastasia Kerensky has been sighted on Northwind, and if her DropShips never returned to Tigress—"

"Then both Kerensky and her DropShips are most likely still here."

"Still here somewhere, and we don't know where." Tara Campbell turned to Captain Bishop. "Captain, send for Brigadier General Michael Griffin. I have work for him to do."

11

Castle Northwind
Rockspire Mountains
Northwind
December 3133; local winter

Brigadier General Michael Griffin had traveled to Castle Northwind on official business before, and he knew enough not to bother attempting to approach it overland. The remote glacial valley could be reached by road, but not quickly. The journey required several hours of travel along the main highway, followed by more hours spent climbing into the heart of the Rockspires on a strip of winding two-lane blacktop, culminating in passage through a heavy-duty security barrier and a final half-hour ascent via the Countess's private driveway.

Over the years, the setting had proved quite effective as a means of ensuring privacy—or at least, that any interruptions would not be trivial ones. Michael Griffin, like most visitors with urgent news to impart, came to Castle Northwind by air.

The pilot of Griffin's VTOL descended below the cloud cover at last. Griffin watched through the window beside his seat as the aircraft made its final approach to the castle.

Even on an overcast day like this one, the vista was impressive. Castle Northwind lay in the most dramatic part of the Rockspire Mountains, where the jagged, perpetually snowcapped peaks had been further scored by the advancing and retreating glaciers during Northwind's most recent ice age. Here, glacial action had scooped a long valley out of the granite, cradling a series of intermountain meadows and a deep, spring-fed lake. The castle stood on the high ground above the lake, with a precipitous mountainside for a backdrop; seeing it, Griffin could understand why the long-ago first Count of Northwind, given the choice of any place on the planet in which to build his principal residence, had chosen this spot.

The VTOL landing pad was separated from the castle by a small wooded hill, for the sake of deadening the sounds of landing and takeoff—and also as yet another measure to discourage casual or unexpected visitors. The early Counts and Countesses of Northwind had valued their privacy, and the current Countess followed tradition, coming here to work when she didn't want interruptions.

Yet, thought Griffin, she had summoned him. The fact left him tense with anticipation. He already suspected the root cause of her summons—he had seen the morning's message traffic from domestic intelligence, and as Prefect, Tara Campbell would have gotten the same report. General Griffin felt a touch of unworthy pleasure underneath the tension and anxiety—Paladin Ezekiel Crow was with the Countess, but she had not asked for the Paladin, she had asked for him. She would have—he hoped—orders for him.

Michael Griffin was not an unperceptive man. He was as self-aware as the next person and by no means stupid. He knew quite well that he had succumbed early on to Tara Campbell's particular combination of courage, beauty, and charm, and he was equally certain that the Countess had never come close to regarding him in a similar light. But it was to him, and not to the Paladin, that she had earlier given the task of holding Red Ledge Pass.

An electric runabout waited beside the VTOL landing pad. The vehicle required no driver, being self-steering over its programmed path to and from the castle, and Griffin boarded it at once. The VTOL pilot had not yet finished his postflight routine; Griffin would send the runabout back to the pad empty, and the pilot could come up to the castle later if their stay turned out to last more than a few hours.

Castle Northwind's butler—an impressive individual who reminded Griffin of a regimental Sergeant Major in mufti was waiting for him at the main entrance.

"The Countess is in the lesser hall, sir. Up those stairs and to the right."

"Thank you," Griffin said, and followed the directions up to a large room—"lesser" only by comparison with the great hall below, which was big enough to contain an entire political rally, if some Count or Countess ever wanted to hold one. This room was considerably cozier, with a thick carpet, a fire crackling on the hearth, and a view of snow-covered mountains through the leaded-glass windows.

Tara Campbell and Ezekiel Crow were working together at a long table covered with folders and printouts and portable data terminals. The Countess's aide, Captain Bishop—another Tara; sometimes it seemed to General Griffin as if half the female twentysomethings on Northwind answered to that name—had another, smaller table off in one corner, with its own data terminal and stack of papers.

The Countess looked up and smiled as he entered the room. "General Griffin! Thank you for coming so promptly."

"Orders from the Prefect do have a few advantages," he said. "I bumped aside five other people and got the next available military VTOL leaving the New Barracks."

"A wise decision," said Ezekiel Crow. "You've seen the intel report?"

"Of course," Griffin said. "It's another reason I moved as rapidly as I did. The prospect of Anastasia Kerensky active again on Northwind is most disturbing."

The Countess ran a hand through her short blond hair, making it stand straight up. "That's probably the understatement of the year. When you add in the stories about those Steel Wolf DropShips never returning home to Tigress, it's worse than disturbing—it's downright scary."

Griffin nodded. "I take your meaning. We have to assume that those DropShips are somewhere in the Northwind system—the question is where."

"It would be handy if we had some idea when they reentered Northwind space," the Countess said. "But with the observation post at the jump point still only working about half the time, we're as likely to have missed them as caught them sneaking in."

Captain Bishop looked up from her workstation's display long enough to ask, "But how do you hide something as big as an entire flotilla of DropShips?"

"With considerable difficulty, I should imagine," said Ezekiel Crow. "But Anastasia Kerensky is daring and resourceful; she will have thought of something."

"They could be lurking on the far side of one of the moons," Captain Bishop said.

The Countess gave her aide an approving glance. "That's a good thought. We can send a couple of DropShips up there as soon as we can spare them, to make a swing around and check for signs of life. But this new piece of intelligence puts Kerensky or someone a whole lot like her down on the Oilfields Coast. And I don't think that the Galaxy Commander is going to stray far from her ships."

"So you believe that she's hidden them here on the planetary surface somehow," Griffin said.

"Exactly," the Countess said. "And we can't look for her on the surface using remotes. There's too many places to look, and it takes an instruction set a lot more complex than 'fly past and report anything not logged on previous flyby.' "

"You'll have to send troops out of Fort Barrett to conduct a reconnaissance in force."

The Countess turned to Ezekiel Crow. "I told you he'd see the point right away." Then to Griffin she said, "You're right—I want a reconnaissance in force. And I want you to be the one who conducts it."

"I'm honored by your trust, my lady."

The Countess gave him a wry smile. "You should be furious with me for handing you another chance to get yourself killed. But the last time I asked you for something impossible, you delivered. Now your good deeds are being rewarded because I'm doing it again."

She paused for a moment, while Griffin heard only the fire on the hearth, crackling and hissing, and the soft but distinct patter of sleet against the window panes. Then she continued.

"General Griffin, I need you to find those DropShips, and quickly. If Anastasia Kerensky has brought the Steel Wolves back to Northwind, she won't stay hidden for long."

PART TWO

Hunting

December 3133–February 3134

12

Balfour-Douglas Petrochemicals Offshore Drilling
Station #47
Oilfields Coast
Northwind
December 3133; dry season

Sixteen 120-count boxes of latex examining gloves.

Another Friday night in sickbay, Ian Murchison
thought as he entered the number into his data pad
and closed the supply cabinet door. In some ways
his situation had changed radically since the Steel
Wolves takeover of Balfour-Douglas #47; in others,
however, it remained much the same. He was still
functioning as a medic, still patching up those indi-
viduals who happened to fall ill or injure themselves
out here on the rig. But now he had a double cord

around one wrist, and a new status to go with it: Bondsman to Galaxy Commander Anastasia Kerensky.

He wasn't certain why she had spared him, when the Steel Wolves had killed all the other drilling station personnel, either in the battle or afterward. For all he knew, she'd wanted a pet, and liked the idea of one who wasn't afraid. He would have been afraid, he thought, if he could have taken the time away from checking the bodies of the station team, but once Anastasia Kerensky had found him, there'd been no point in cowering when it looked like she was going to kill him whether he cowered or not.

Now he was mostly bored. The Steel Wolves had proved to be a disgustingly healthy lot, and if it weren't for their habit of fighting each other on a regular basis, often for reasons Murchison found frankly incomprehensible, he wouldn't have had any injuries to tend either. Today had brought him a broken wrist and a knife wound, both from the same altercation. Murchison had wanted to write up an aggressive-incident report form, but everybody involved had seemed to regard the affair as settled. He'd written up the form anyway after they left. Habit and routine were wonderful things.

Now he was reduced to inventorying medical supplies for his entertainment. He wondered if his position as a Bondsman—in which, as he'd had it explained to him, his value to the Galaxy Commander derived from his medical expertise—extended to requisitioning replacements for expended stock. He gave an inward shrug. He could always ask. After that, it would be up to Anastasia Kerensky what the Wolves did with the request.

He'd barely begun working on the list when he heard footsteps in the corridor outside his office, and recognized the Galaxy Commander's distinctive tread. Speak of the devil, Murchison thought, and he enters without bothering to knock. Or she does, in this case.

Anastasia Kerensky could not have been back long from her mainland expedition, but she had already changed out of her plundered hiking gear and into her favored black leathers. She had also returned her hair color to its previous glossy black with deep red highlights. Murchison smiled to himself at the speed of the reversal. Life as a mousy brunette had clearly not suited Kerensky's temperament at all.

"Bondsman Murchison," she said, as soon the office door had closed behind her.

He got to his feet. He wasn't certain what the customary etiquette was for their relative positions, but it never hurt to pay the standard respect to authority until instructed otherwise. Besides, being within arm's reach of Anastasia Kerensky gave him a "be ready to move out of the way in a hurry" feeling, and keeping on his feet helped him to deal with it.

"Galaxy Commander," he replied.

"I trust that the good health of the station continued in my absence?"

"Aye. No illnesses, only minor accidents, only one fight." He extracted the aggressive-incident report form from his desk and handed it over. "Warriors Jex and Zane."

"That Trial has been coming for some time," she said, with no visible surprise, and scanned the report. "Nothing permanently disabling—good. Who won?"

"Not my place to ask, ma'am. So I didn't."

He heard a snort of suppressed laughter, and struggled against the urge to shudder—Kerensky's good humor was as frightening as the rest of her. Eyes bright with what Murchison sincerely hoped was amusement, she said, "A Clan Wolf medic would have at least been curious."

Amusement or not, he was damned if he was going to grovel. "We are who we are, Galaxy Commander."

"True," she said. "You, for example, are discreet and conscientious. You are also my Bondsman." She indicated the pair of cords around Murchison's wrist. "Do you understand what those mean?"

"Not completely."

"Then I will explain. These are a symbol of your probationary status. When both of them are cut, you are no longer *isorla*—part of the spoils of war—but *abtakha*—an adopted member of the Clan. In the old days, mind, your situation would not be so fortunate; it was only Warriors who could become *abtakha*. But the Steel Wolves move with the times—so your present status is not necessarily a permanent one."

She looked at him as though expecting a reaction. His mind caught on two words—probably the ones she'd meant him to notice. "Not necessarily?"

"Complete a task for me successfully, and I will cut one of the cords."

For a long moment, Ian Murchison said nothing. He had to remind himself that Anastasia Kerensky

was dangerous in the extreme even without her Steel
Wolves to back her up—capable of killing him where
he stood if she needed to, or if she thought it might
be amusing. But she respected fearlessness and appreciated honesty, and those qualities had kept him
alive so far. "Are you making me an offer, Galaxy
Commander?"

"Are you trying to negotiate with me, Bondsman?"

Her smile was dangerous enough to make anyone
hesitate. But there was no backing down now. "No,
ma'am. But not all jobs are the same. If I knew that
I couldn't do one, I'd turn it down and wait for
another."

"Even though there might never be another?"

"Yes, ma'am."

She raised a disbelieving eyebrow. "Are you that
afraid of failure?"

"Not of failure, Galaxy Commander."

There was another long pause, during which Anastasia Kerensky regarded him with a steady, considering expression, and he wondered if she had
decided to kill him out of hand, anyway. At last,
however, her expression changed from consideration
to grudging approval.

"You are a stubborn and stiff-necked bastard,
Bondsman Murchison. If I can make a Wolf Clansman out of you, you will fit in well."

He supposed it was meant as a compliment. "If
you say so, ma'am."

"I say so." He couldn't tell if the faint sound she
made then was a private laugh or a resigned sigh.
"Very well, Bondsman Murchison. I will tell you
what task I have for you, and you will tell me yes

or no. But one thing"—she held up her right hand, and now it had a knife in it—"if the answer is no, you will not speak of this conversation elsewhere, on pain of death. Are we clear?"

"We're clear, ma'am." He watched the knife go away. "What is it that you want me to do?"

"I want you to find me a man." She paced restlessly the few steps across the width of his small office and back again, and he took note. This was something that disturbed her more than she wanted to say outright. "Or a woman. I do not know. But this—person—if he or she exists—has been in contact with Jacob Bannson."

"Bannson Universal Unlimited? *That* Bannson?"

"Yes."

"I thought The Republic had clipped his wings a while back. Told him to stay in Prefecture IV and keep out of trouble."

Anastasia Kerensky's lip curled. "As you may have noticed, not everybody is playing by The Republic's rules any longer. I do not; neither does Jacob Bannson. But that does not make us natural allies, no matter what he may think."

"I can see that, Galaxy Commander."

"Do you? Excellent. Then you can see why I do not want one of my Wolves in his employ. A divided loyalty is never good."

"No, ma'am," said Murchison dryly, then wondered if he had gone too far. Anastasia Kerensky was not so unsubtle that she would fail to notice irony.

To his relief, she laughed. "You would know, Bondsman. So I ask you: Is this a task you can accept?"

"If I were a soldier," he said slowly, thinking aloud, "I would have to say no. I would have oaths and responsibilities that took precedence. But I'm not a soldier. I'm a medic, and all the oaths I've ever sworn have had to do with that; and you aren't asking me to break any of those."

Anastasia Kerensky remained silent, letting him work it out, and he continued, "If you wanted me to find someone who was spying for Northwind, I'd have to say no; this is my homeworld and I have a duty to it, even if I am a medic and not a soldier. And then you really would have to kill me, so it's just as well you aren't asking me to do anything like that."

"Just as well," she agreed. She sounded more amused, he thought, than angry. "Go on, Bondsman."

"But Jacob Bannson is no friend of Northwind's that I ever heard of," he said, "and I never swore any oaths to Bannson Universal Unlimited. I'll hunt your spy for you, Galaxy Commander."

13

*Balfour-Douglas Petrochemicals Offshore Drilling
Station #47
Oilfields Coast
Northwind
December 3133; dry season*

When the Steel Wolves took over the offshore drilling rig, Anastasia Kerensky claimed as her own the living quarters of the station manager—who, being dead, made no objection. She disliked being separated from her DropShips, but the Wolves needed an operational headquarters nearer to the continent.

Her new quarters had other advantages as well. The manager had liked his luxury, or at least as much as he could get of it on an oil rig. The cabin had an extra-wide bed instead of a narrow ship's bunk, and a private bath almost as big as the bed. Nobody had to worry about a shortage of bathing and drinking water here; the drilling rig had an entire ocean of salt water to distill it from. At the end of a long day—which this one had certainly been— she appreciated the chance to fill the enormous tub with hot water and bath soap, and lie there soaking until the all the tension ebbed away.

Anastasia relaxed in her bath, thinking of her agreement with Ian Murchison. She had not lied when she said that the medic would make an excellent Wolf; she approved of the way he refused to allow himself to be afraid. And good medics were always an asset to any force.

She took a sip from the heavy crystal tumbler sitting on the wide edge of the tub. That was another advantage to her current quarters: the former occupant had liked good liquor, and had kept his cabinet supplied with an excellent private stock. Not the Terran vodka she preferred when she could get it, but local brews—and Northwind, she had decided, would be a planet worth taking for its distilleries alone. The amber whiskey had a taste like knives and burning embers, and a label in a language she didn't recognize; she would remember it, though, when they left this place and had all of Northwind to plunder.

Footsteps in the main cabin interrupted her thoughts. A loaded slug pistol lay on the rim of the tub next to the whiskey; she had the weapon in her hand and aimed before the door swung all the way open.

At the sight of the newcomer, she relaxed a little. It

was Nicholas Darwin, whose undeniably handsome presence was yet another advantage to having her private quarters on the oil rig's managerial level. She did not lower the pistol, however, but smiled at him over it.

"If you had been an enemy, I would have killed you as soon as you came through the door."

"If I had been an enemy," he replied, also smiling, "I would have waited on the other side and killed you when you came out."

She laughed, not putting down the pistol. "But since you are not an enemy, waiting is too difficult for you?"

"The sight of a Galaxy Commander armed and dangerous in her bath is too rare a privilege not to be taken advantage of."

"See an advantage and take it." She rose smoothly from the tub, the slug-pistol in her hand. It was a move that could have been awkward, and Anastasia was vain enough to be pleased with herself that it wasn't. And the effect on Nicholas Darwin of bathwater and soap bubbles sluicing off her naked body as she stood was all that could be desired. "I like the way you think. Bring the whiskey and come with me to bed."

She stepped past him. He followed; when she turned, she saw he had brought a bath towel with him, as well as the whiskey bottle and the empty tumbler.

She raised an eyebrow. "Why the towel?"

He set the bottle and the glass on her bedside table, and unfolded the towel. "Mutually beneficial tactical maneuver," he explained. "You get to not have soapy water soaking into the bedsheets, and I get to touch you all over."

"Good plan." She set the slug-pistol down on the bedside table next to the whiskey. "I like it."

She liked it, as matters turned out, very much indeed. It was fortunate that nobody still living berthed on this level except for the medic, Ian Murchison, and that his room was at the opposite, or low-status, end of the managerial corridor. That put him too far away to hear most noises, and as for what he might overhear anyway . . . well, he was not likely to talk.

Some time later, she lay happily exhausted with her head on Nicholas Darwin's shoulder, watching the play of light and color on the cabin's ceiling, relaxing into a brief pleasant moment free of rank or position or struggle for power. Such moments never lasted long, but one of the good things about taking a regular bed partner was the fact that they came at all.

There was a picture on the ceiling, a changeable electronic flat poster, glowing dimly in the low ambient light. She inferred from its presence that the late manager's taste for luxury didn't include sex, or he would have had a mirror there instead—or at least pictures of an inspirational variety, rather than shifting landscape views.

She said so aloud, lazily and already half asleep. Darwin chuckled.

"Maybe he didn't need them." When he was relaxed, his dialect slipped downward out of true Clan precision into the looser speech of Tigress's non-Clan community—a reminder that he was freeborn, the product of random genetic mingling, and not carefully bred from the Clan's DNA stock and brought to life in the iron wombs. "Or maybe he got turned on by landscapes."

"It takes all kinds, I suppose."

She lay there watching the images cycle overhead: waves caught in the moment of crashing onto a sunlit beach; vast rolling fields of tall grain awaiting the harvest; a gray stone castle cupped in a mountain valley.

"I like that picture," she said. She was growing sleepier now, relaxing against Nicholas Darwin's side, lulled by the steady rhythm of his heartbeat. "The castle."

"I read a story about it in a magazine, while we were stuck playing tourist in Fort Barrett. It belongs to the little Countess, the one who rides the *Hatchet-man* 'Mech."

She yawned. "I want one just like it someday."

"Take Northwind, and you can have that one."

"And see if the little Countess has a mirror over *her* bed." She smiled at the thought, and still smiling, drifted off to sleep.

═══ 14 ═══

Fort Barrett
Oilfields Coast
Northwind
December 3133; dry season

It didn't take long for Will Elliot to settle in to life as a Sergeant. The amount of work was about the same, but now it wasn't enough simply that he himself not screw up. He had to make certain that ten or more other people didn't screw up either. Truth to tell, he didn't find it all that hard. He'd been doing much the same thing with Jock Gordon and Lexa McIntosh ever since basic training.

Will had feared, in fact, that his promotion, and the distance that it would put between him and his two best friends, would result in their inevitable estrangement. His worries, however, proved unnecessary. To their own surprise as much as anyone else's, Jock and Lexa also made Sergeant shortly after Will's own elevation in rank.

Lexa in particular had contemplated her new stripes with foreboding. "That proves it," she said. "Something bad is going to happen."

"What makes you say that?" asked Jock.

"Because, otherwise, who in their right mind would ever have promoted the likes of us? I'm the bad girl of Barra Station, and you—let's just say that when your mother was filling out the order form, she didn't check the box for the extra-brainy option."

Will frowned at them both. "You made it through Red Ledge Pass, and you made it through the battle on the plains. As far as the new recruits are concerned, you're old and brave and very, very wise. Don't disillusion them."

Within a fortnight, however, the early-morning routine at Fort Barrett was broken by a small VTOL craft setting down on the headquarters pad, and Will began to suspect that Lexa had spoken the truth. The arrival of visitors at headquarters was not in itself ominous; people came and went all the time, even here at the restful end of nowhere. But an hour or so later, a heavy cargo-lift VTOL came over, its tarp-shrouded burden dangling beneath, and landed on the fort's main pad—which would not have been unusual either, except that the timing was all wrong for any of the regular milk runs from New Lanark. And an off-schedule cargo arrival, especially in conjunction with an important visitor, was bound to mean something special.

How special, Will soon discovered. He was heading past the main pad, on his return from taking the morning muster reports to headquarters and bringing back the daily staff briefing, when he saw that the VTOL's heavy cargo was now uncovered and mobile: a *Koshi* BattleMech, with hunched back, bulky arms and forward-thrust cockpit, standing on the pad while its pilot took it through the bends and stretches of what was probably a posttransport checkout routine.

Will paused to watch. It looked from the outside as though the 'Mech was engaging in a stately series of mechanical calisthenics, bending and flexing its metal-and-myomer limbs, testing the balance and stability of its twenty-five-ton bulk. The long flight from New Lanark must have been a strain on both the 'Mech and on the VTOL carrying it; only because the *Koshi* was one of the lightest 'Mechs would the aircraft have been able to lift with it at all.

The last time Will had seen that *Koshi* was at Red Ledge Pass, when the Highlander infantry held up the Steel Wolves' armored column for thirty-six hours, buying time for the Countess of Northwind and Paladin Ezekiel Crow to organize the main defense. The rider of the *Koshi* had been heart and brain of that holding action, always there to back up the beleaguered infantry where the action was thickest, dealing out death to the Wolves' infantry when they threatened to overrun Highlander positions.

The series of self-tests done, the *Koshi* came to the rest position and shut down. A minute or so later, the pilot left the cockpit and descended via the entry ladder. Even from the far edge of the pad, Will recognized the man's ginger brown hair and erect posture. Fort Barrett's important visitor was Brigadier General Michael Griffin—the pilot of the *Koshi* at Red Ledge Pass, and senior officer in charge of the infantry's holding action.

Now Griffin had come to Fort Barrett. Not for a quick visit, either, if he'd brought the *Koshi* with him.

At noon in the Sergeants' mess, Will's suspicions were confirmed. He was talking with Master Sergeant Murray—who, while inhumanly spit-and-polish under all circumstances, had proved considerably more affable than Will had thought he could be—over the day's lunchtime meal of fish and chips with sponge cake for dessert.

"I saw General Griffin warming up the *Koshi* this morning," Will said.

"It's an impressive machine." Murray gave Will a suspicious look. "You're not one of those foot soldiers who secretly wishes he could be riding a 'Mech, are you?"

Will shook his head. "Me? No. Too big, too noisy, too cramped . . . I'm all for living and dying in the out-of-doors. They'll put me into a box soon enough."

"Too true."

"The Colonel is good, though . . . I remember the Pass." Will finished up the last of his fish-and-chips and turned to the sponge cake. The battered fish had been excellent, made from the fresh local catch; the sponge cake tasted like it had been made by somebody who'd read a description once and missed the point. But enough chocolate frosting could make anything edible. Will chewed, swallowed, and continued,

"What's he doing here at Fort Barrett, do you know?"

"Regimental headquarters has some work for us. The Colonel's come down here to do a reconnaissance-in-force, and we're going to be supplying the force."

"Somebody really likes putting him out at the sharp end," Will said. "And us."

"You ought to know how that works by now, Elliot: Show them that you can walk on water, and the next time around they give you deeper water with higher waves in it."

"Aye. What are we going out looking for?"

Murray smiled. "You ought to know—you spotted her first yourself."

"What . . . ?"

Then Will remembered the celebratory dinner at the Riggers' Rest, and the woman who had reminded him, as he was dropping off to sleep hours later, of Anastasia Kerensky. By the time he'd awakened the next morning, he'd convinced himself it was only a coincidental resemblance. He'd turned in a report anyway, expecting it to be filed somewhere and promptly forgotten, not—

"All this on my say-so?"

"I'm afraid so, son." Murray chuckled. "No, not really. The bright boys and girls in Regimental intelligence undoubtedly had an entire box full of puzzle parts they fitted together to get the big picture. You just gave them the missing piece."

15

The DropShip *Cullen's Hound* would lift from Tara DropPort in twenty-four hours, and Di Jones was scheduled to ride. She had her ticket and her papers in hand, she'd checked aboard her few items of luggage—she'd traveled light, as always, and in any case she hadn't been able to bring with her on this mission the only thing she possessed that she truly valued, her *Hatchetman* 'Mech. Now she had time to kill before *Cullen's Hound* took its departure and, thanks to Jack Farrell, damn his one remaining eye, she had an appointment to kill it with.

She met Farrell in the DropPort's main concourse, a huge dome-covered expanse with transit links to the rest of the port and to the city of Tara proper. The concourse wasn't as full of people these days as it would have been before the collapse of the HPG net, but it was still thronged with people. Casual interstellar travel had become a thing of the past—its existence had depended, more than most people realized, on rapid communications and a general peace—but the need to carry stored media or hardcopy news and correspondence from system to system had kept the DropShips coming to Northwind.

Jack Farrell sat on a bench near the outbound to Tara transit gate, reading a one-sheet printout of the day's top stories from the *Northwind Intelligencer*. Di had a chance to read the top headline—COUNCIL PASSES ECONOMIC AID PACKAGE—before he folded up the one-sheet and tucked it into his jacket pocket.

"Di," he said, rising to greet her. "Nice to see you again."

"Farrell. Wish I could say the same about you." The statement was only a half-truth. She had to admit that he was a dangerously good-looking man, even—or especially—with the black eye patch. She wished that the sight of him didn't make her so twitchy, even after all this time.

As always, he seemed unaffected by her insults. "Let's find a better place to talk. Maybe local intelligence has this whole building stuffed full of eyes and ears, and maybe it doesn't, but I don't feel like taking the chance."

"Back into the city?"

"Works for me," he said, and headed off with long

strides for the outbound to Tara gate, leaving her to follow.

One light-rail ride and two hoverbus transfers later, they ended up sitting opposite one another in the back booth of a corner café in the working-class section of Tara. The air in the café was rich with the smells of sausages and steak and bacon, and the background chatter of the noontime crowd was punctuated by the pop and sizzle of hot fat.

Farrell ordered two luncheon specials—today's offering was a mixed grill—and a pot of coffee from the booth's touch-screen menu. The coffee was strong, black, and fresh; the cream came in a pottery jug.

Di frowned at Farrell's high-handed assumption that he knew what she wanted without asking, but stopped short of actual protest. She'd missed breakfast in the rush to get her luggage checked aboard *Cullen's Hound* twenty-four hours before departure. Now she was hungry, and she wasn't going to let the fact that One-Eyed Jack Farrell knew her likes and dislikes keep her from enjoying lunch.

Of course, there remained the business discussion to be gotten through as well. Farrell began it, while they drank coffee and waited for their specials to arrive.

"How did the meeting with your target go?"

Even here—in a place as unlikely to be bugged as any in the city—he didn't mention Anastasia Kerensky's name. There was no point in drawing attention to themselves by speaking the name of the woman who had led the Steel Wolves to within hours of striking at the city's heart.

"Eh. Turned me down flat."

"It was always a possibility," Farrell said. "Those people don't think like us."

"I didn't meet any of 'those people.' Just her."

"She's one of them, never fear. Crazy like all the rest."

"If you say so." Di wasn't sure exactly what she thought about the meeting with Anastasia Kerensky. The woman's refusal had caused her to feel frustration, yes, but also respect. It was the latter sentiment that had prompted Di to let fall the bit of info about the mole in the Steel Wolf command—which was something she was definitely not planning to tell Farrell about, or Jacob Bannson either. "She doesn't want to owe anything to anyone, that's the problem."

Farrell's response was a lazy smile. "Takes one to know one, darlin'. Not that you're crazy or anything."

"And this is the point where I remind myself that I can't kill you right now because we're both working for the same guy."

"That's right," he said. The waitress brought them their luncheon specials, and he paused for a moment until she had gone away again. As soon as the woman was safely back behind the counter, he dug into his bacon and sausages and continued, "I wouldn't worry about the no-deal thing. The boss didn't hire you to be his traveling saleslady."

"Good thing, because she sure wasn't buying." Di finished her first cup of coffee and poured another. "On the other hand, the boss should appreciate my travel diary."

Farrell raised his eyebrows. "Lots of pretty pictures?"

"And lots of notes. What about you?"

"I'm still waiting for the right moment to approach my target." The raised eyebrows gave way to a disgruntled expression. "At least yours is an honest villain—"

"Villainess."

"All right, villainess—who isn't lying about anything and isn't on anybody's side but her own. I wouldn't trust mine any farther than I could throw a BattleMech."

"I wouldn't trade with you, that's for sure. Your target gives me the cold shivers—make a wrong move, and you could end up deader than yesterday's breakfast."

"Worried about me, love?"

Di shook her head vehemently. "Thinking that I'd be real sorry if somebody else put a knife into you before I got around to doing it myself."

"Relax, sweetheart." Farrell leaned back and gave her his most annoying and lascivious grin. "I'm saving myself for you."

16

Night had fallen over Balfour-Douglas #47, drawing Ian Murchison once more out onto the observation deck for a few minutes of quiet solitude. He leaned against the deck's metal railing and relaxed as best he could in the night air, his skin cooled by the breeze blowing across the open water. Neither of Northwind's two moons was up, but the sky held a myriad of stars spread out against velvet black. Down below, in the water swirling around the legs of the drilling platform, floating bioluminescent jellyfish drifted and sparkled.

Murchison was tired, not least from the unremitting state of low-level anger and anxiety that he knew was worth his life to express, and the double cord on his left wrist was a constant irritant.

There was also the matter of his deal with Galaxy Commander Anastasia Kerensky.

He wanted to ask himself what had possessed her, but he knew better. The Steel Wolves' commander believed, for some reason—for all he knew, it could be his open and honest face—that he was steady and reliable. More to the point, she saw in him someone steady and reliable who had not been part of the Steel Wolves' military machine since the day he was decanted, someone with a fresh eye to look for signs of duplicity and betrayal.

My eye's so damned fresh it's never going to see anything, he thought bitterly. I'm not looking for a needle in a haystack, I'm looking for one needle in a whole bin full of needles.

The idea depressed him. Maybe Anastasia Kerensky would believe him when he said that he couldn't find the traitor because all her Steel Wolves blurred together, for the most part, into one indistinguishable and largely unpleasant mass. More likely, she would think he was lying.

The murmur of voices around the corner of the observation deck broke into his thoughts, and stirred his curiosity in spite of his unhappy mood. He edged closer, keeping well out of sight, until he had drawn near enough to recognize the voices of Star Colonel Nicholas Darwin—the Galaxy Commander's favorite—

and Star Captain Greer. Both men ranked high in Anastasia Kerensky's councils, which sufficed to lift them out of the general run of Warriors in Murchison's recall.

Greer's voice was the first to resolve into words. ". . . longer do we go on waiting like this? We need to bring up the DropShips and attack."

"You have the wrong man for that question."

"Do I? You are Kerensky's darling."

Darwin's voice was slightly lower than Greer's, and tinged with amusement as well as with a faint difference in the accent. "If you think that means I have any influence on the Galaxy Commander's decisions, you do not know her well at all."

Greer's voice took on an ugly note. "And you know her better than you let on. I am not blind; I have seen you going about her work. If she had not given you the keys—"

Murchison eased forward, keeping himself in darkness, until he could see the two men standing outside the door to the stairwell. The small light over the door illuminated them: Darwin dark and compact; Greer tall, pale, and rawboned.

Their body language at the moment reflected the antagonism he'd overheard in their speech. Greer was trying to loom over Darwin, while Darwin was leaning back against the railing in a manner clearly meant to look annoyingly relaxed. The tense set to his shoulders, however, gave his posture the lie.

Murchison considered clearing his throat or dropping a writing stylus—anything to make a noise and break the tension. After reflection, however, he remained silent. If Anastasia Kerensky had made him into a spy; then he would play the spy and do nothing, only listen.

Darwin said, "What would you have me say to her, then? 'If I may distract you for a moment, Galaxy Commander, Star Captain Greer desires to know when it will please you to lift the DropShips?' " He laughed. "And when she says, 'Star Captain Greer will know that the DropShips are lifting when Star Colonel Darwin learns about it and tells him so,' do you think I am stupid enough to ask her anything more?"

"I think you are a nasty patch of freeborn scum, and the only good you are to the Galaxy Commander comes from your—"

"Be careful." Darwin's voice was quiet now and not at all amused. "You insult Anastasia Kerensky, which is foolish. And you insult me, which—considering that you and I are standing here alone together without witnesses—is even more foolish."

Star Captain Greer took a step forward. "You are threatening me."

"Well, yes. I thought you would notice it eventually."

Greer made an inarticulate noise of disgust and slid his right hand down over his left forearm. When the hand came up into view again, twenty centimeters of knife protruded from his fist—not one of the clasp knives that Murchison had long been accustomed to seeing in use on the rig, but something double-edged and leaf shaped, a serious fighting knife. The metal was subdued, a matte black color that neither reflected nor shone in the light; the edges alone, where the blade had been sharpened, glittered.

"Then I will send the Galaxy Commander the part of you that she likes best," Greer said. "In an extremely small box."

"You are welcome to try, Star Captain." Darwin pushed away from the railing and widened his stance, flexing his knees and bringing his hands up to waist level, palms open and empty. He made little "come hither" motions with his fingers. "You are very welcome to try."

Greer didn't answer. Not with words. He turned his left side to Darwin, empty hand up. The hand with the knife he lowered behind him, switching his grip on the blade from point up to point down. Then he stepped forward, his left hand grasping Darwin's left arm high up as he turned and brought the knife in his right hand slashing up and cutting Darwin's arm.

Unfazed, Darwin turned and grabbed Greer's left hand with his own right, squatting at the same time to duck under his opponent's outstretched arm. Then he straightened, and Greer's left arm, extended over Darwin's shoulder, broke with a crack when the elbow bent the wrong way. The knife clattered to the deck plates as Greer's other hand went lax from the shock.

Darwin stepped back, turned to his left, and pushed. Greer fell away from him, back pressed against the observation platform's railing. Greer was a lanky man; the top bar came up no higher than his waist.

"Good-bye," Darwin said, and spun again, his foot high, smashing out with a side kick to Greer's chin. The man vanished backward over the rail.

Darwin stooped and picked up the knife from

where it had fallen. He looked at it for a moment, then dropped the weapon over the railing into the sea below.

Murchison faded back into the darkness and took the opposite-side stairway back up to his quarters. He didn't bother undressing and going to bed. Not at all to his surprise, his beeper sounded almost as soon as he had closed the door behind him. He went down to sick bay and—as he had expected—found Nicholas Darwin waiting for him outside the closed door.

"Star Colonel," he said, "is there a problem?"

"An injury, Bondsman Murchison."

"Where's the patient?"

"Here."

"Come in, then, and let me see to it."

Murchison opened the door to sick bay and flipped on the lights. With the improved illumination, he saw that Star Colonel Darwin had his right hand squeezing hard on his left biceps. Blood stained his bare fingers, and the sleeve below the gripping hand was dark with blood.

"Take a seat, sir," Murchison said. "What do you have?"

"A cut."

Murchison pulled on a pair of examining gloves. "Let's take a look."

The Star Colonel took away his hand. Already the blood between his fingers was dark red and clotting. Nothing was spurting out of the wound—that meant no arteries had been cut, which was good.

"Is this your favorite shirt?" Murchison asked, reaching for a pair of trauma shears. A moment later, when the area was exposed, "Let me clean that up for you, sir. It looks like you'll have to have a few stitches. Is your tetanus immunization up to date?"

"Of course it is. Now hurry up."

"Yes, sir. Now, if I didn't know better, I'd say that looked a lot like a knife wound. The Galaxy Commander wants any weapons injuries logged and reported."

"That won't be necessary," Darwin said. "There's no need to log or report such a minor accident. I'm leaving in the morning on a tour of inspection, and all that paperwork would just make for delay."

"Yes, sir," Murchison said again. He pulled a laceration tray from the cabinet and unsealed it on his working table. "Now this is going to hurt a bit. . . ."

The Star Colonel's dialect had slipped a moment ago, Murchison thought. Darwin's word choice had veered away from the annoying overprecision that the Clans favored in their speech, and his accent had thickened slightly. He was clearly more upset than he let on; more upset than the wound itself should have merited, given the typical reaction of Murchison's other Clan patients to similar injuries. Star Captain Greer—the *late* Star Captain Greer—had hit a nerve in Nicholas Darwin somehow. Several nerves, if the resulting pain had proved bad enough to warrant a trip over the side.

Murchison finished the patch-up job and sent Star Colonel Darwin away to bed. Probably, for a change, to his own—Darwin's footsteps, instead of continuing in the direction of the Galaxy Commander's quar-

ters, headed toward the stairs leading back down to
the oil rig's next lower level, where most of the Steel
Wolf officers on board had their compartments. Murchison, meanwhile, sat alone in the sick bay for quite
a while, thinking.

=== 17 ===

The New Barracks
Tara
Northwind
January 3134; local winter

The city of Tara marked the start of the new year
with a grand military review presenting the defense
forces of Northwind to the civilian population. Planetary Legate Finnegan Cochrane stood in the reviewing stand as the people's representative. Paladin
Ezekiel Crow and Countess Tara Campbell were, for
once, among the participants in the parade rather
than the dignitaries watching it: their *Blade* and
Hatchetman 'Mechs, and Captain Tara Bishop's *Pack
Hunter*, brought up the rear of the parade, coming
after the infantry units and the armored cars, the

tanks and the artillery, the converted Agricultural and Mining 'Mechs.

The parade had at last made its ponderous way through the streets of the city and back to the New Barracks. Tara and Crow had taken the first opportunity to change out of their 'Mech combat gear and back into working uniform, and had left Captain Bishop behind to handle the final details of parade cleanup—one of advantages of having an aide, Tara reflected, was that you could occasionally shift the boring stuff onto somebody else for a few hours.

She and Crow walked side by side in companionable silence across the open ground between the Armory and the main Barracks complex. After a while the Paladin said, "Please tell me that I won't have to listen to bagpipes again for a very long time."

"You mock our great cultural heritage," said Tara, laughing. "Everybody on Northwind likes the sound of the bagpipes."

"I don't. I'm not certain I would even call it music."

"It's not music—not just music, anyhow." She pulled her face into an exaggeratedly serious expression. "According to my old cultural anthropology tutor, the sound of the pipes is 'an auditory stimulus designed to evoke an altered state of consciousness.' He meant that it gets the battle fury of our ancestors roaring in our veins."

"*My* ancestors, however, have decided that it gives them a headache."

The back-and-forth joking had taken them up the steps and into the main bachelor officers' quarters of the Barracks complex. Tara, in her persona as Prefect of Prefecture III, had a suite of rooms there as well; the door opened with a touch of her hand to the lock. She entered the suite, Crow following, and waved the Paladin to a guest chair. Then she went over to the sideboard, which held a heavy crystal decanter etched with the regimental crest and a set of matching tumblers. The decanter was full of a dark amber liquid.

"It's past noon," she said, "and I've spent the past six hours marching—marching, would you believe it!—in a *Hatchetman* BattleMech. Care to join me?"

Crow shook his head. "Thank you, but no."

"That's right. I forgot. You don't." She poured herself a modest one finger of whiskey and stoppered the decanter. Taking the chair across from Crow, she stretched out her legs and contemplated the toes of her boots. Her mood was changing; she was coming down off the post parade and bagpipes high, and crashing hard. "And the people on Northwind would be shocked if they found out I did. Don't ever let anyone decide that you're the people's darling, my lord Paladin. It's damned wearing."

"You carry it off well."

"I've been practicing since I was barely old enough to walk." She sipped at the whiskey. Crow said nothing. She said, "They depend on me, and I worry all the time that it's not going to be enough."

"Last summer—"

"Was only the first time. They're going to keep on coming—if it isn't Anastasia Damn-her-eyes Kerensky it's going to be the Swordsworn or the Dragon's Fury or some other group of heavily armed opportunists." She took another sip of whiskey. The strong fumes crawled up her nose and clawed at her throat as she drank. "And it doesn't matter how impressive we look on parade, we don't have enough men and women under arms to keep on fending them off."

"If you're concerned about the size of the Northwind garrison, you could always withdraw the Highlander units from planets such as Small World and Addicks."

"And leave those planets bare? No."

He shrugged. "It was a thought. If you're unwilling to call in the off-world forces, you'll have to recruit at home."

"We've been. But it takes time. And I don't know how much of that we've got."

"Have you considered hiring mercenaries?" he asked.

"Not really."

Distaste must have shown in her face and voice because he looked at her curiously. "Why not?"

She was silent for a moment, marshaling her thoughts. "I'm—uncomfortable—with the idea of negotiable loyalties. I can't imagine it for myself, and I suppose I have trouble believing that such people are trustworthy."

"Not exactly a reasonable position, considering the history of your own regiments."

"Touché." She acknowledged the hit with a wry smile. The Northwind Highlanders had fought for pay on worlds all over the Sphere, making a name for themselves as tough and competent mercenaries long before they returned to defend a world of their own. "It takes a kind of honor, I suppose, to hold to the letter of a contract in spite of all opposition. But setting aside my personal prejudices—which I'd do in a heartbeat if I thought it might help me protect Northwind—won't do me any good as long as I've still got to deal with the problem of money. Hiring mercenaries takes a lot of ready cash, and with the economy as shaky as it is, I don't know if I could persuade the Council to take the plunge."

There was another stretch of thoughtful silence. Then he said, "There is a workaround."

"Tell me."

"If you are willing," he said slowly, "I can engage mercenaries using my authority and funding as a Paladin of the Sphere, and Northwind can accept their aid without having to negotiate with them—or pay them—directly."

"Can it be done quickly? There's no point, if it can't be."

"If I let the word propagate by fast DropShip, we should get a response within a month or so if we get a response at all."

"All right, then." She exhaled on a long sigh and tossed back the last of the whiskey in her glass. "Do it."

18

In spite of the winter season, the day-to-day weather on the Oilfields Coast of Kearney was warm. The planet's equator was so close here that there wasn't much difference between one season and another in any case—instead of spring, summer, fall, and winter, the climate varied between wet and dry. This was the middle of the dry season, and no rain had fallen since the end of September.

The noonday sun beat down from a cloudless sky on the men and vehicles assembled near the gates of

Fort Barrett. Anyone who was hot now would be hotter still when they were marching with a full pack—or strapped into the cockpit of a 'Mech.

Brigadier General Michael Griffin, who would be riding the 'Mech in question, looked at the assembled force with a critical eye. Griffin's *Koshi*, repaired and rearmed after taking heavy battle damage at Red Ledge Pass, would be at the rear of the column, where the dust stirred up by its heavy footfalls would not destroy visibility for the other units. He would be shadowed, as he had been at the battle for Red Ledge Pass, by his aide-de-camp Lieutenant Owain Jones, in a BE701 Joust tank.

The rest of the force was a mixed lot, made up of units chosen for what Griffin hoped would be the optimum combination of strength and mobility: a reinforced company armed with a mix of Thunderstroke Gauss and laser rifles, plus a heavy weapons platoon of Cavalier battle armor; an additional scout/sniper platoon mounted on Shandra scout vehicles; and a pair of attached Balac Strike VTOL aircraft.

This assignment would be harder in some ways than defending the pass had been. On that occasion, necessity had chosen his forces for him—a mix of what was ready and what could be spared—and his task, while difficult to carry out, had been simple enough to understand. There had been only one road by which the enemy could come, and only one thing for Griffin to do about it, a brutal business, but not, ultimately, one that taxed the mind.

This time, though, was different. For a reconnaissance in force he needed mobility, in order to search out the enemy; but—because the most likely way of finding the enemy was by running into them—he also needed to bring along sufficient firepower to fight his way out of trouble. Too light a mix, and he would risk being chewed up before he could get word back to headquarters. Too heavy, and either the noise and dust of their advance would alert the enemy to run away, or they would encounter overwhelming numbers of the enemy and lack the speed to escape.

Griffin hoped he'd judged it right.

"Here's the situation," he said aloud. He had a field map of the Oilfields Coast unrolled and lit up on the front chassis of the Joust tank, currently parked near the left heel of Griffin's BattleMech. The task force's company and platoon leaders had gathered at the feet of the *Koshi* for the briefing.

"As most of you probably know," Griffin continued, "we've had a sighting of Galaxy Commander Anastasia Kerensky in downtown Fort Barrett. Regimental intelligence says that Kerensky is unlikely to be onplanet without some kind of backup from the rest of the Steel Wolves—and those DropShips that landed last summer in New Lanark may have left Northwind, but they never showed back up on Tigress. Headquarters wants to know where they are, so we're going out hunting."

He tapped the red dot on the map that marked the location of the Kerensky sighting. "We'll be doing an expanding square search, taking this for our center point."

Lieutenant Jones looked at the map. "That's a lot of territory to hunt for one person in," he observed.

"We're not looking for Kerensky anymore," Griffin

told him. "We're looking for those DropShips. Which are a hell of a lot bigger and harder to hide."

The major who commanded the reinforced company asked, "What about all the parts of the search area that are open ocean?"

"We'll be doing periodic overflights with the attached Balacs, but our best bet is going to be the coastal flatlands south of here." He lit up the area in question on the map. "It's empty territory, more or less—the soil's not fit for growing anything and the rocks don't have any minerals in them worth digging out."

"When we find the DropShips, what do we do then?"

"In an ideal world, we'd send headquarters a message marking their location, then hunker down somewhere outside of the blast zone and let people who have more firepower than we do take care of things from there." Griffin turned off the map and rolled it up. "But since this world is far from ideal, we'll probably find ourselves fighting our way out of trouble at some point before we're done."

He handed the map to Lieutenant Jones, then stepped over to the entry ladder of the *Koshi*.

"All right, people—it's time to mount up and head out."

=== 19 ===

Balfour-Douglas Petrochemicals Offshore Drilling
Station #47
Oilfields Coast
Northwind
January 3134; dry season

Ian Murchison spent the rest of a sleepless night thinking hard about the task Anastasia Kerensky had assigned to him, and about what he had seen and heard that late night on the observation deck. The two were not necessarily connected—a man's behavior could have many reasons—but someone who was looking for a single bent needle in a bin full of straight ones could do worse than to start out by examining the first specimen that looked off-true.

When Star Captain Greer missed breakfast as well

as the morning head count, his absence—and subsequent failure to appear—caused a certain amount of disturbance. Ian Murchison soon found himself being questioned by one of the other Steel Wolf officers, a Star Captain named Jonath. Murchison couldn't remember if he had ever seen him before or not.

The interview seemed to be mostly a formality; Jonath came up to Murchison's office in order to ask his questions, rather than dragging Murchison down to the drilling station's one-cell brig. As an acknowledged Bondsman of Anastasia Kerensky, Murchison had more or less free run of the oil rig in any case. There were some places, such as the communications room, or the access points for the motor whaleboat and the emergency life rafts, that had guards posted, and he was routinely barred from those. But otherwise . . . this far out from land, where could he run?

In keeping with this general attitude, Star Captain Jonath's questions were the routine inquiries of a man seeking to round out an already established picture.

"Where were you between"—Jonath consulted his data pad—"1830 and 0600 last night?"

"Here. Finishing up the day's paperwork." It sounded as if dinner the night before had been the last time Star Captain Greer was on public view. Murchison had been there as well—it seemed that the Wolves found it less trouble to allow a Bondsman to eat with the general mess than to treat him as a prisoner and feed him separately—which gave him a bit of protective coloration for the lies he was telling now. It was just as well, he reflected, that his habit of taking a late-night stroll up on the observation deck to clear his mind before bed had never become general knowledge among his captors. "Then I closed up the sick bay and went to my quarters for the night."

"Did you see Star Captain Greer during that time period?" Jonath asked.

"No," said Murchison.

He waited for a follow-up question about being called back to sick bay to patch up Star Colonel Darwin, but none came. It looked like the Star Colonel had not reported his fight with Greer to anyone, which Murchison found more than a bit odd. Based on his admittedly limited experience with Steel Wolf Warriors and their fights, under normal circumstances Darwin would have been far more likely to tell the whole story to the first person who would listen, and the second and third persons as well.

If, that is, the altercation had been a legitimate fight, by whatever rules the Clans used to determine such things. The fight itself had undoubtedly been fair—Greer had been the bigger man, as well as being armed when Darwin wasn't, and had made the first aggressive move. However, Murchison remained more than half convinced that the killing of a fellow officer done by night and kept secret afterward qualified as murder or something like it even by Wolf standards.

"It could be death by misadventure," he volunteered to Star Captain Jonath, thinking that he might as well throw some general confusion into the air.

"What do you mean?"

"Accidents happen, and this isn't a forgiving environment. People can stumble in the wrong place, or fall at the wrong time, and go over the rail into the water and not come back up."

Jonath looked a bit disconcerted. "Bodies float, surely."

"Not for long," said Murchison. "The big hungries come and get them."

"Big—I see."

"If you check the drilling station logs, you'll find that a worker named Ted Petrie vanished the same way back in February of '32." Murchison didn't add that fifty feet of heavy chain had vanished the same night, or that Petrie had had a record of sexual harassment and petty theft and was not beloved of his workmates. Nothing had ever been proven, after all.

"I will check that."

Jonath closed his data pad and left. Murchison stayed at his desk and waited until enough time had passed for the Star Captain to have left the managerial level entirely. Then he retrieved a data pad of his own from a desk drawer and wrote in it for some time. When he was done he left the office, locking it behind him, and went in search of Anastasia Kerensky.

He found her, as expected, in the main operational control room of the oil rig. Several other Steel Wolf officers were present as well—not Darwin, though, which Murchison considered was probably significant. If he didn't want his injury to be discovered, he would have needed to find an excuse to absent himself from the Galaxy Commander's company.

The Steel Wolves had transformed the rig's control room into a military command center. Not much effort had been required—mostly, they had moved in a number of portable communications and data consoles, and had covered the main work table with a large tri-vid field map of the Kearney continent. Murchison glanced at the map in passing and recognized the Oilfields Coast, with what looked like Balfour-Douglas #47 picked out in red. The presence of several other red dots, not far away, puzzled him for a moment, since Balfour-Douglas had no oil rigs in that area that he could remember. He put the question aside; he had, for the moment, other and more pressing thoughts.

Anastasia Kerensky looked up from the map as he entered the control room. "Bondsman Murchison. Should you not be in your sick bay?"

"I have the accident and casualty reports you requested, Galaxy Commander," he said, and proffered his data pad.

She raised an eyebrow. "You work fast."

"It's nothing conclusive—I don't have the personal resources to follow up on a lot of the things I've listed—but some of the data might be worth looking into further."

"Your work is not unappreciated, Bondsman Murchison." She took the pad. "I will look into the matter myself—careless accidents should not be allowed to hamper our operational efficiency, and those responsible will be punished appropriately."

The comment, Murchison thought, was as good as a dismissal. He gave what he hoped was an appropriately nonservile but respectful response and made a quick and silent exit. He wanted to be well out of range before Anastasia Kerensky read his report, in case the Galaxy Commander was the sort of person who liked to shoot the messenger.

The New Barracks
Tara
Northwind
January 3134; local winter

Paladin Ezekiel Crow had his quarters in the New
Barracks, in the building designated for housing
long-term important visitors. He occupied a suite of
rooms very much like the ones reserved for the Prefect whenever he or she was on-planet, and that Tara
Campbell was now occupying: one inner room for
sleeping and one outer room for working and social-
izing, with sanitary facilities off the first room and a
cooking and dining nook off the second, all done up
in a bland offend-no-one style.

Crow knew the look well; he'd been living with it,

in one local version or another, for most of his diplomatic and military career. Sometimes the default inoffensive furniture was made of polished natural hardwood, and sometimes of matte black molded resin, and sometimes of chrome; in some places the local style called for deep crimson and bright green and royal blue, and in others for beige and gray and ivory. Good taste on Northwind demanded natural wood, and paint and fabrics in subdued but not drab colors at the cool end of the spectrum; the Prefect's official quarters were another variation on the same theme.

The only difference was that Tara Campbell had added a number of personal touches to her quarters—a picture of her parents in a silver frame; an ornamental brass lantern from Sadalbari; chairs and other items of furniture not from the general mold, but much like those which filled the rooms at her family's mountain castle. Crow had made no such changes to his own quarters. He never had done, not since Chang-An burned. Making a mere assigned place into something like home had always seemed disloyal to him somehow, a way of saying that something else could take the place of what was lost. He was not going to do that. If he could not bring his old home back, the least he could do was not forget it.

Crow also had an office assigned to him, not in the two-century-old New Barracks, but in the massive and much older structure known as the Fort. He had considered telling his visitor to meet him there, but in the end had decided that—since he would not be acting as a representative of Northwind—the Fort would be too official a location.

His quarters weren't much better as far as seeming official went, but he didn't want to handle the negotiations over drinks in a bar, either. People did that when they possessed money without possessing authority, or when they had things that they wanted to hide. He was a legitimate guest on Northwind, and a Paladin of the Sphere. He had nothing to hide.

The communications console gave the double beep that meant the building's front-door security was on the line. He picked up the handset.

"Crow here."

"Security here, sir. We have a Jack Farrell here at the information desk who says that he's expected."

"He's here on business," Crow said. "Send him on up."

"Yes, sir."

A couple of minutes passed—time enough to cover a hallway and an elevator and another hallway at a walking pace—and the doorbell buzzed. Crow opened the door, and saw that it was indeed One-Eyed Jack Farrell (as the merc was known to members of his profession) waiting on the threshold.

"Come in," said Crow.

Farrell entered. The man was well-groomed and well-dressed but—to a trained eye—not nearly as respectable as his clothes would suggest. The black eye patch was a giveaway; even if the damage had been too severe for a prosthetic, the man could have gotten a cosmetic implant. That he preferred not to, Crow thought, argued that the eye patch must be a combination of advertisement and signature.

Though Crow had never met Farrell before in the flesh, the merc's name and reputation were known throughout the Inner Sphere. One-Eyed Jack had the name of a tough and ruthless fighter, but—on the positive side—neither Farrell nor the units under his command had ever backed out of a lawful contract, nor were they prone to looting and rapine. When Crow had last heard of them, Farrell and his mercs had been in Jacob Bannson's employ; but that had been before the HPG net went down, when Bannson was still trying to extend his business empire into all the farthest corners of The Republic of the Sphere.

Crow led the way to the living and work space. The chair and the couch and the low table between them were general issue, not as comfortable or as attractive as the deep, leather-covered guest chairs and the generously proportioned sofa in the Prefect's quarters. Crow took the chair, leaving Farrell to the end of the couch.

"My compliments on your security," Farrell said. "My name got checked against the invite list once at the main Fort entrance and once at the gate of the New Barracks before I ever got to the people downstairs here."

"The Highlanders are good. And they're careful."

"But they have a problem they can't handle," Farrell said, "or I wouldn't be here. I heard that you were hiring for some local work—and as it happens, my wayward children and I are currently between engagements and close enough to be available."

"How close, exactly?"

"The entire force can be here inside twelve days."

"That's . . . prompt," said Crow. His dubiousness must have shown on his face, because Farrell—as eager, perhaps, to obtain a contract as Northwind, through Crow, was to offer one—hastened to explain.

"They're currently holding at the jump point. Pure coincidence—I came to Northwind to check on the news from around The Republic and get a line on where we might find work next, and the first thing I heard when I hit the bulletin boards was that you were in the market."

"Yes." Crow was careful not to appear eager. Nothing was more likely to sabotage a deal in the making than seeming to want it too much. "We're considering it."

"So." Farrell leaned back in the couch. "What's going on that's too much for the locals?"

"They're overextended," Crow told him. "Not through their own fault; they've been tasked with defending other worlds in Prefecture III as well as Northwind."

Farrell made a *tsk-tsk* noise. "Somebody was being ambitious."

"The Senate and the Exarch didn't anticipate that this planet would become a target as well when they gave the Prefect her orders. She lost a significant portion of her on-planet effectives during this past summer's campaign, and the recruitment and training of replacements will take some months. If she is not to strip other worlds of their protection, then she must hire you—or someone like you—to fill the gap."

"We're talking garrison duty, then."

"Essentially. Good pay for—if you're lucky—very little work."

"It's one way to rest up," Farrell said. "Is Northwind good for the money?"

"The Republic of the Sphere, through me, is good for the money. Is that enough for you?"

One-Eyed Jack Farrell grinned. "Paladin Crow, you've hired yourself some mercs."

===== 21 =====

DropPort
Tara
Northwind
January 3134; local winter

Twelve days after his conversation with One-Eyed
Jack Farrell, Ezekiel Crow watched Farrell's mercenaries disembark from their DropShip at the Tara
port. He had an excellent view of the proceedings,
standing as he did beside Tara Campbell in the VIP
observation lounge of the DropPort's main
concourse— a luxurious private room, all deep carpet
and glass windows snugged up under the concourse's overarching dome. In times past, when the
volume of traffic in and out of the DropPort had
meant DropShips arriving and leaving several times

a day, the lounge had been a gathering place for passengers who considered themselves too well-off or too important to mingle with the crowds in the general waiting area. Today, as on most days since the collapse of the HPG network, it had been empty until the Countess and the Paladin arrived.

Outside the windows, the sky over the DropPort was an intense winter blue. In the dazzle of noonday sunlight the main cargo hatch of the grounded DropShip gaped open into an impenetrable black shadow.

The mercenary infantry left the ship first, marching in formation down the ramp of the cargo hatch. Crow knew that this was standard procedure—it was the fastest way to move men and women in large groups. Allowing the mercenaries to go one by one down the passenger ramp would take hours, and would create a disorderly mess that would take more hours to sort out. All the same, the steady flow of distant figures, anonymous in their dark fatigues, oppressed him.

It wasn't as if he didn't know why. Liao had started out this way—the landing of a small force, meant only to restore order, or so at least they claimed—and it had ended with blood in the streets and Chang-An burning. Had there been a point all those years ago, he wondered now, when one person with the gift of foresight could have put out a hand and said, "Stop!" and prevented everything?

"You're brooding," said Tara Campbell. The Countess of Northwind was wearing a winter uniform, made of wool against the cold wind that blew outside, and her short, spike-cut hair gleamed bright gold in the light through the windows. She had a tendency to twist and pull at bits of that hair whenever she was feeling uncertain; it occurred to Crow that he hadn't seen her doing so for quite a while. She was growing into her position as Prefect, then, which was good—the Senate and the Exarch had worried, at first, that her unexpected elevation to the suddenly empty post would overwhelm her. "I'm supposed to be the one with doubts about all this, not you."

"Memories," said Crow.

She knew enough of his past, he thought, that she would understand what he meant. He had told her last year about finding his parents dead and everything lost in the bloodbath that had become known as the Betrayal of Liao. It was rare for him to speak of the past, even obliquely, but Tara Campbell had a way of drawing confidences from him.

Down below, out on the landing field, the infantry had gotten themselves clear of the DropShip and into lines for boarding transport vehicles to take them to their assigned barracks. The cargo ramp was now spewing forth other stuff than soldiers: hoverbikes, all-terrain vehicles, armored cars, tanks, and self-propelled guns; all the muscle and sinew of mechanized war. The vehicles, armor, and artillery drew up in ranks on the tarmac as they emerged. Farrell's mercenaries, Crow thought, were a fearsomely well-equipped group.

"It won't happen," Tara Campbell said, breaking into his silence. "What you're thinking about. This"—she gestured at the field below—"is all about stopping it before it happens."

"I know," he said. "And I know that hiring merce-naries was my suggestion in the first place, and that I argued for it until I convinced you. But still." He looked out over the growing array of military ma-chinery with a growing sense of ill-defined unease. "One worries."

The mercenaries' BattleMechs were offloading from the DropShip now. The smaller ones came first—although "smaller" was a relative term, since even the least of them towered over the big self-propelled guns. Crow spotted first a *Spider*, then a *Firestarter*, then a *Mad Cat III*. Nobody was making do with Industrial or Agricultural Mods here; all the mercenary force's 'Mech's had been designed for bat-tle from the start. Then the last of the BattleMechs emerged from the DropShip's shadowed interior: a *Jupiter*, one hundred tons of heavily armored slaugh-ter and destruction, One-Eyed Jack Farrell's own deadly darling.

"They're certainly a well-equipped bunch," Tara Campbell observed. A wistful expression passed over her features. "I wish the Council loved its own Regi-ments enough to vote us money for hardware like that. Hell, I wish there was money enough available that I'd feel right about asking for it."

She stepped away from the window with a sigh. "I suppose it's time to go shake Mr. Farrell's hand and bid him welcome to Northwind. I hope he wasn't expecting to get a formal reception."

"His kind of people seldom do," Crow said.

══ **22** ══

*Balfour-Douglas Petrochemicals Offshore Drilling
Station #47
Oilfields Coast
Northwind
January 3134; dry season*

Evidence. Damning evidence, spread out across the
screen of the data console in Anastasia Kerensky's
quarters.

The medic Ian Murchison had given her nothing
more than a name, an account of a disturbing—and
unreported—incident, and a conjecture. That had
been a good move on Murchison's part, Anastasia
thought, reminding her that his Bondsman status
didn't give him any room or authority to dig further,

followed up by throwing her detective challenge right back into her lap.

And it had been a clever move as well. Murchison had slipped out from under responsibility by denouncing the Galaxy Commander's known favorite, thus forcing Anastasia to carry out the rest of the investigation herself.

She was the only person on #47 with a high enough security override authority that she could track messages sent out over her name, or with her access codes; and she was the only person who could swear definitely that some particular message was one that she had never sent.

Once she had found the first such message, the rest came much more easily. She was able to track the use of those access codes to set up hidden mailboxes, and from the mailboxes she was able to find records kept in them and—foolishly!—never erased. Carrying out a search like that was not a knack most people would expect Anastasia Kerensky to have. She was all Steel Wolf Warrior, and Warriors were supposed to be above such things.

Tassa Kay, though, had an un-Wolflike interest in learning all sorts of unseemly skills. She had learned the rudiments of this one from a temporary lover several planets back. Anastasia had needed almost two weeks to uncover what her old bedmate could have brought to light inside a few minutes, but that did not matter. She had taken the time, and now she had the proof.

Now to wait. Nicholas Darwin had been away inspecting the DropShips all this while. That was yet another point in support of Murchison's theory:

Darwin could pass off a healing knife wound as an injury gained during that period. He would be coming back today, though, and sooner or later—sooner, if she were not where he could easily find her in the oil rig's public spaces—he would come to her quarters.

She was ready for him. She would wait.

She had dressed for the occasion in Tassa Kay's boots and leathers. The choice was fitting, she thought. She had been playing at Tassa Kay when she first met Nicholas Darwin, and she had been playing at Tassa Kay when she brought him home to her bed. She should be playing at Tassa again now, for at least this one more time.

One more time, she thought, and never Tassa Kay again?

That was tempting, but in her heart Anastasia knew better. She might need Tassa Kay again sometime, and it was not her way to throw out a good knife because she'd been fool enough to cut her hand with it.

She poured herself a tumbler of the late drill rig manager's potent liquor, then sat on the edge of the bed not drinking it. After a while footsteps sounded outside in the corridor—she tensed, then relaxed—and Nicholas Darwin entered.

Anastasia saw him again as if for the first time: the compact, muscular body; the dark skin that had always so pleasantly surprised her with its smoothness under her touch; the bright black eyes and the laughing mouth. He had been the best of all her lovers in so many ways, a match for her in temper and in stamina, with but a single flaw. . . .

She set down her tumbler of whiskey, rose from the bed, and greeted him with a kiss.

"How are things on the DropShips?" she asked, pulling away before the kiss could deepen into something more. More would distract Darwin, which was good; it would also distract her, which was not.

"They are doing well. All the modifications are holding, and the ship captains report ready to lift at any time."

"Good." She took his hand and led him to the edge of the bed, pushing him on the shoulder to make him sit down. "That will do for a summary. We can go over the details later."

Anastasia knelt on the bed behind Nicholas, with her arms wrapped around him and her lips close to the skin of his neck. She let her hands tease at the collar button of his shirt—the garment was Clan warm-climate issue, the fabric light and breathable but strong, made to resist rips and tears.

"What are you doing?" he asked. His voice sounded amused, warm and rich with anticipation.

"Unwrapping you," she said.

She had the collar button undone, and moved on to the second button, her fingers teasing and tickling. Her teeth nibbled at his ear.

She continued in a whisper. "No way to play if the wrapping is still on."

She undid the third button, then the fourth, and ran the fingernails of her left hand across the bare skin underneath. At the same time, she tickled the upper curve of his ear with her tongue, making him gasp a little with surprise and pleasure. He had nicely shaped ears, close to his head and not over large, and his skin tasted pleasantly of salt.

He laughed. "Missed me, then, while I was away?"

"Yes," she said, and grabbed with her trailing left hand at the collar of his partially unbuttoned shirt.

With one sharp motion she jerked it down to midchest, pinioning his arms to his sides. Her right hand brought the point of her dagger up against the side of his throat, tight against the skin over the carotid artery.

"Do not move," she said. "Do not even think of moving."

"What—" He paused, drew in a shaky breath. "Why?"

"How long have you been in Jacob Bannson's pay, Nicholas?"

Silence. And a pain in her gut, that he made no attempt to deny her accusation. He had to know, then, that proof existed, and that if anyone ever found the proof—as she had done—it would be damning.

She pressed the dagger in a little bit tighter. "How long?"

"Four years."

Four years . . . that was before she ever came to Tigress and challenged Kal Radick for the Steel Wolves. She supposed she ought to take consolation from the thought that Darwin's treachery had not been a personal betrayal. At the moment, she did not feel especially consoled.

"Why?"

"For the money. Bannson pays his informers well."

"You betrayed the Steel Wolves to Jacob Bannson for money?" Her dagger didn't move. She let all of her incredulity pour into her voice. "What does a Steel Wolf Warrior need with *that*?"

"Nothing."

"Then why—?"

"Because with enough money," Darwin said, "a man can choose to be whoever he wants to be. Wherever he wants to be. Life as a Warrior in Kal Radick's Steel Wolves was better than life as an unemployed street rat in the Four Cities, but it was not really a choice."

"What do you mean—'not really a choice.' "

He gave a faint sigh. "You wouldn't understand."

"You have *that* right," she said.

She struck with the knife, cutting deep and across, severing the carotids and the jugular in one blow.

"I do not understand."

23

The New Barracks
Tara
Northwind
January 3134; local winter

After greeting One-Eyed Jack Farrell at the DropPort, Ezekiel Crow and Tara Campbell returned to the New Barracks, first by official vehicle and then—after leaving the vehicle and its driver at the main gate— on foot. The winter afternoon by now was moving on toward dusk. The sun hung low near the crests of the distant Rockspires, and shadows stretched out long on the ground.

As they walked, Crow pondered the fact that the Countess of Northwind had not liked Jack Farrell at all. She had been impeccably polite, of course, as only a cradle-trained diplomat could be—Farrell had probably never noticed the difference—but Crow had seen Tara Campbell's genuine warmth and could tell when it was missing.

He noticed that he had been looking at her without speaking for several minutes, admiring how the dark gold of her eyebrows and eyelashes contrasted with her porcelain-fair complexion, and the way small tendrils of her close-cropped platinum hair curled against the nape of her neck. He looked away again quickly. It would not do to have her catch him gazing at her like an obsessed stalker or—even worse—a lovestruck adolescent.

Maybe it was already too late. Tara Campbell darted him a quick sidelong glance and said, almost hesitantly, "Are you dining at the Officers' Club tonight?"

"I hadn't decided yet."

In actuality, he knew that he was going to follow his usual practice of heating up one of the assortment of packaged meals that he'd bought from the Barracks commissary and currently kept stored in his kitchen nook. But he did not say that. Instead, he waited to see what would happen next—because things had, undeniably, started to happen.

"We could—if you like—dine in my quarters." Tara Campbell's cheeks were faintly red. "I'll cook."

"I'd be honored," he said.

She was still blushing—which was surprising, since he hadn't thought anything embarrassed her. "Don't expect anything spectacular," she warned him. "I know how to make exactly three company dinners, and the kitchen staff at home would laugh at every single one of them.''

He went with her to her quarters, where she at once began pulling meat and assorted vegetables out of the kitchen's tiny refrigerator, rice and oil and spices out of the overhead cabinet, and cooking utensils out of the storage space beneath. With a bit of amusement, he realized that she'd actually had her spur-of-the-moment invitation planned out well in advance—like a general planning out a military campaign.

The kitchen nook wasn't big enough for him to offer assistance and do anything except get in the way. He contented himself with leaning against the edge of the doorway and watching her at work. She had a chopping board and a heavy knife, and was busy cutting up the meat—he wasn't certain what kind it was, except that he didn't think the flesh had come from any of the usual Terran stock meat animals. Something indigenous and probably reptilian, at a guess. He wasn't going to pursue the matter; he'd eaten stranger things than lizard in the course of his diplomatic and military career.

With the cubes of whatever it was set aside in a bowl, she moved on to the vegetables: onions, garlic, squash, and peppers that Crow recognized, and something purple and tuberous that he didn't. When all of those were chopped, she began heating the cooking oil in a big sauté pan, and set the rice to steaming in a separate pot.

"It's a Sadalbari mixed curry," she said in response to his question, after a desultory conversation on mil-

itary matters had flagged and left him casting about
for another subject. "I had it so many times while I
was posted there' that I thought I was sick of it, and
then I missed it after I got home. So I found some
recipes and worked at it until I got it almost right."

She paused long enough to add the cubed meat to
the now hot oil, filling the kitchen nook with the
sound of furious sizzling. "Or as close to right as I'm
ever going to get it, anyhow. It's kind of like politics
that way."

It was, he thought, an interesting comparison, as
well as a telling character note. Aloud, he asked,
"How's that?"

"Never having anything be all the way right. Just
as close to right as you can manage with the ingredi-
ents that you've got." She shifted the cooking meat
around in the sauté pan with a wooden spoon,
frowning a little as she did so. "There's a reason why
I'm a soldier first and a politician a long way
second."

"Some people," he commented, "would say that
there isn't that much difference between politics
and warfare."

"That's because they don't have jobs that make
them do both." She added seasonings to the cooking
meat—salt and coarse black pepper and a generous
pinch of a pinkish-brown powder that smelled like a
combination of star anise and sandalwood. The air
in the kitchen bloomed with sudden flavor. "I do,
and I tell you truly, Paladin, I'd sooner fight a
pitched field battle any day than try to negotiate a
peacetime budget with the Council."

She tossed in the chopped vegetables—more loud sizzling resulted, and a cloud of steam—and covered the sauté pan with a lid. Then she turned down the heat. "Now we let it alone for a while."

The Countess of Northwind put her used cooking utensils into the dishwasher and wandered off into the living room area. Crow followed her. She sat down at one end of the wide, leather-upholstered couch, and gestured to Crow that he should take a seat next to her. He was more than willing to comply.

"The last thing in the universe I'd ever want," Tara continued, "would be your job. All politics all the time, even when you're fighting."

"A Prefect who hates politics," he said with mild— almost fond—amusement. "Such hardship."

She scowled at him. "I do this job because it's my duty, and because there isn't anybody else. What's your excuse?"

"It's something that I *can* do, and do well." There was nothing to be served here by false modesty, not when his statement was demonstrably true, so he didn't bother. "And it needs to be done—and done again, over and over—to keep The Republic of the Sphere from falling into complete disorder."

"I understand."

Tara's voice was full of a multitude of unasked questions and unstated acceptances, and he knew that she must be thinking of Chang-An burning, and of everything that he would have lost in its destruction. Her blue eyes, bright with sympathetic tears, spoke of kindness, and perhaps of something more. Moved by a sudden impulse—it had been a long time since anyone had offered him a moment of fellow feeling—he moved closer on the couch, then bent his head and kissed her.

She kissed him back.

She was not hesitant at all now, but firm and decisive, like a general seizing a battlefield advantage. He wondered, in a moment of blurry reflection, if such an exchange of mutual comfort had been as long ago for her as for him; then he gave up on analytical thought altogether. His hands were unbuttoning her uniform tunic almost on autopilot; her hands were equally busy undressing him.

The curry burned, and they ended up dining some hours later on flash-heated meals-in-a-box from the Barracks commissary, but they didn't care.

$$=== \mathbf{24} ===$$

Benderville
Oilfields Coast
Northwind
February 3134; dry season

The narrow road wound southward along the coast from Fort Barrett. At first the task force passed through small towns built up around inexpensive retirement communities for Kearney's senior citizens and beach houses for vacationers from the continent's interior. These thinned out as the city fell more than a couple of days' civilian travel behind. Instead, the road ran between fishing villages next to canning and freezing plants, where rusty trawlers unloaded their catch at the long wharves. Those, too, became further and further apart, until even the paved road gave out, replaced by a one-lane track of sandy clay, graded—it looked to Will Elliot—once or twice a year.

The progress of the task force slowed as the road got worse. Will and his fellow scout/snipers spent most of their time showing around pictures of Anastasia Kerensky to shopkeepers, local law enforcement officers, and (at the suggestion of Will, who was small-town born himself) old people on front porches and small children at play. So far, their inquiries had not produced any useful results—although the children and the elderly, at least, had proved full of acute observations about the doings of their friends and neighbors.

"It's because they're the ones who don't have most of their minds taken up with work and all," he said to Jock Gordon and Lexa McIntosh over field rations at the noonday break. The rations today featured barley-and-mutton soup from a self-heating can, just the thing for the dry-season heat. "They see things that most people miss."

"If you can get them to talk," said Lexa. A reminiscent expression played over her face. "Half the stuff that went on in Barra Station when I was a kid, none of us *ever* talked to the grown-ups about."

"That's because you were a menace to society," Jock said.

"Still am," she said. "Only difference is, the regiment gave me a pretty new laser rifle to menace with."

"I suppose that makes you the expert," Will said. "So how do we get the kids to open up about things they aren't mentioning to the grown-ups?"

"Have you considered bribery?"

"In case you hadn't noticed, we're not exactly millionaires here," Jock pointed out.

Lexa gave a scornful snort. "There's other things besides money." After a thoughtful pause, she added, "Of course, money almost always works."

In the event, bribery turned out not to be needed after all. They came that evening to the smallest town yet. Benderville was nothing more than a scattering of decrepit houses plus a combined fuel station and general store. Half a dozen children rode the district hoverbus every day to and from a consolidated school five towns back up the road. The task force halted there for its evening meal at the same time as the school bus dropped off its passengers and turned around to head back north.

Dinner this evening was more self-heating soup, this time chicken and rice. As they had at noon, Will, Jock and Lexa hunkered together in the lee of the Joust tank. After a few minutes, Will became aware of a skinny towheaded kid with his textbooks done up in a string backpack, standing a few feet away and shifting his weight from one foot to the other as he watched the soldiers eat.

When Will caught his eye, the boy turned red and visibly worked up the nerve to speak. "You from Fort Barrett?"

"Aye," said Will.

"Whatcha doin' way out here?"

Will glanced at Jock and Lexa. Lexa nodded—go for it, her expression said; this one's a talker. "Looking for someone."

"Are they lost?"

Will shook his head. "They know exactly where they are. But we don't know where to find them."

The towheaded kid's eyes got bigger. "Are they bad people?"

"Nasty as they come," Lexa said, with an evil grin that suggested she knew all about nastiness.

"Oh," the boy said, in a more subdued tone.

"Don't worry," she said. "We kicked them hard the last time. Right, Sergeant Elliot?"

"That's right, Sergeant McIntosh," said Will.

To the boy, he said, "We need to know if they've come back, so that we can kick them again." He took out the sheet of paper with the artist's photorealization of Anastasia Kerensky's current appearance, unfolded it, and showed it to the boy. "One of the people we're hunting for looks like this—have you seen her anywhere?"

The boy shook his head.

"You may not have seen her at all, just her vehicle."

The boy shook his head again. "Nobody's come this way except you guys." He paused, and his brow wrinkled. Will could almost hear him thinking. "Does an aircraft count as a vehicle? Because I've seen one of those a couple of times."

Will put aside his can of soup and stood up. "I think the General wants to talk with you."

"I don't know—maybe I'd better—"

Lexa snaked out an arm and grabbed the boy before he could run. "Oh, no you don't."

"Hey!"

"Don't worry," Jock said. "She isn't going to hurt you."

"He's right," said Will. "Let him go, Lexa."

Will turned back to the boy. "Nobody's angry with you, and General Griffin is a nice man." Moved by inspiration, he added, "He pilots the *Koshi*."

The boy's eyes went to the BattleMech, looming nine meters tall at the center of the task force's small encampment. "Can I see it if I go with you and talk to him?"

"It'll be hard to miss it. Come along."

The boy followed Will over to where General Griffin, his aide Lieutenant Jones, and the company commanders were eating their own cans of self-heating soup conveniently next to the foot of the *Koshi*. Saluting, Will said, "General Griffin, sir. This young man says he's seen aircraft."

Griffin got an eager gleam in his eye distinctly at odds with his spit-and-polish soldierly appearance. "How many?"

The boy swallowed nervously and said, "Only one, both times."

Griffin said to his aide, "Jones . . . your data pad." He took the pad, then tapped and wrote on it with the attached stylus until he had called up pictures of several different aircraft. Will recognized all of them as known Steel Wolf configurations.

"Did they look like any of these?" Griffin asked the boy.

"It's hard to tell. They were a long way off." He pointed. "But I think it was that one."

Griffin, half to himself and half to the boy, said, "Excellent. Now we know we're on the right track. If there's anything you'd like—"

The boy's eyes grew very bright. "Can I see inside your BattleMech?"

The General suppressed a smile. "I think we can manage that."

═══ **25** ═══

The recon force set out the next morning from Benderville. The encampment began stirring into motion
a couple of hours before the usual time, while the
sky was dark, with only a pearly glow of coming
sunrise along the inland horizon. As Sergeants, Will,
Jock, and Lexa were all awake in the early-early.
They stood by the supply truck drinking flash-heated
tea—strong and sweet with sugar and condensed
milk—from their mess cups prior to waking the rest
of the infantry.

"Responsibility," said Lexa, yawning widely, "is a

bitch. Last to bed and first awake and behaving myself all the time to set a good example . . . why did I let you talk me into letting them promote me like this?"

"Because you trust me to have your best interests at heart?"

"Lemme think about it." She paused for a moment, then shook her head. "Nah. Can't be."

Jock said, "It was the uniform—you couldn't resist him in it. I could see you looking at him and drooling."

"Go on. As if I'd take a chance on losing a perfectly good buddy that way." She finished the last of her tea. "Must have done it out of the kindness of my heart. Somebody has to teach the new kids which end of the laser rifle the pretty red light comes out of."

"That'd be you, all right," said Will. He looked at his watch. "Time to wake the children up for breakfast."

He and his fellow Sergeants began moving among the soldiers huddled in their sleeping bags. "Wakey wakey," he chanted as he passed from one drowsing bundle to the next. "We're burning daylight."

The harangue was a familiar one from his days in Basic Training, though he'd never expected to find himself on the delivering end of it. Jock's voice, coming from further off, provided a rumbling echo, punctuated by Lexa's cheerfully obscene exhortations from over on the other side of the camp: ". . . and pull on your socks! Save it for Fort Barrett, boys, we've got work to do."

After a hurried breakfast of hot tea and cold ra-

tions, the task force began to move out. The Balac
Strike VTOLs went first, rising from the ground in
swirls of dust to head out in the day's search pattern,
one VTOL covering inland, and one the seaward sector. As they climbed they dwindled to bright dots
against the pink sky of dawn, catching the light of
the rising sun like a pair of fast-moving morning
stars.

The aircraft would be ranging ahead of the column, on the track suggested by last night's encounter. Will hoped that the boy had given a fair
representation of the truth. He hadn't acted like a
liar, but even the most truthful of youngsters wasn't
above shading or coloring a tale, sometimes not even
on purpose.

The noise of the lifting VTOLs faded, and was replaced with the sound of other engines stirring to
life: the troop trucks, the scout cars, the Joust tank,
the General's *Koshi*. Will saw the last of his squad
onto their Shandra scouting vehicles, then mounted
up himself.

The graded dirt road south of Benderville dwindled in short order to a rutted track, the sandy
ground to either side held in place—barely—by
sparse brown grass. A hot wind blew out of the
coastal interior. Sand came with it, stinging against
bare skin, drifting into the folds of cloth and bends
of flesh, sifting down into the cracks of instruments
and machinery. As the day wore on, the constant
sand and grit would be worsened by the passage of
the task force's vehicles, and by the heavy footsteps
of the *Koshi*. Will thought longingly of the hot show-
ers in Fort Barrett; he knew that by evening he would

be grateful for the chance to sluice himself off with a bucket of lukewarm water.

"Another lovely day at the seashore," he said to the squad corporal, over the rumble of the Shandras' engines. "Just remember, there's daft folk in the big city who'll pay good money for an experience like this."

26

The New Barracks; Tyson and Vanvey 'Mech
Factory
Tara
Northwind
February 3134; local winter

Ezekiel Crow woke up scared.

He had returned to his own quarters, at the close of
the previous evening's interlude with Tara Campbell, in
a state of such near-euphoria that he had been hard-
put not to show it. It would not have done at all for
a Paladin of the Sphere to have been caught laughing
aloud in delight as he walked through the halls of the
visiting officers' quarters. The same elevated mood had
carried him off into a sleep filled with pleasant dreams.

The next morning, however, brought with it an

emotion close enough to terror to leave him shaking. He had not realized the extent of his self-imposed isolation until part of it went away. It was as if he had been living behind walls of thick glass that muted everything outside. Now a window had opened, letting in a world of sight and sound and smell more intense than he had ever believed existed.

Distracted and thoughtful, he made himself tea in the kitchen nook, standing barefoot in his black pajamas and measuring out the tea leaves with careful hands. When the water sang in the kettle, he poured it over the leaves in the pot and waited, brooding, while they steeped.

He was not certain that he could handle this. He had ideals, he had goals, he had a hard-bought knowledge of all the things that needed to be done—things that those who were currently supposed to do them weren't doing well, and sometimes weren't doing at all. None of the careful plans he'd worked out over the years since his first life died in the rubble of Chang-An had taken into account something like this.

He didn't know if it could last. He didn't know if he should want it—if he should even allow it—to last. His life had no room in it for hostages to fortune. He had worked hard over the years to keep himself unattached—to people, to places, to anything—for the sake of the freedom of action that comes from having nothing to lose.

All would be well, even now, if only he hadn't been made aware of everything that he was missing.

He took a clean cup from the cabinet. Like the

teapot, it was of inexpensive local make, its appearance plain bordering on ugly. He'd bought the tea set when he came here, and he would leave it behind when he left. No hostages; no attachments.

He poured a cup of the fragrant tea and drank it slowly, still thinking. When he was done, he set the cup aside and went over to the communications console. There he typed in a message to Tara Campbell:

My lady—

Please do not take it amiss that I am out of touch today. I find I must go inspect the 'Mech conversion program in place at Tyson and Varney. It would be lamentable if a hitherto excellent and reliable firm were to begin slacking off for lack of supervision. Believe me when I say that I am looking forward to speaking with you again this evening, after the day's work is finished.

Respectfully,
Ezekiel Crow

He sent the message, then proceeded to wash and dress and put on clothing for the day. He wore his usual plain civilian clothes; they helped to keep him unnoticed and out of trouble.

That done, he headed out in the direction of Tyson and Varney, where the plant manager was surprised to get an unscheduled visit from Northwind's current Paladin-in-Residence. Nevertheless, he happily took Ezekiel Crow on a tour of the hangar where the next generation of battle-modified IndustrialMechs was under construction. As Crow had expected—in spite of having deliberately implied otherwise in his letter to Tara Campbell—everything at the factory continued on track and in order.

Over tea and sandwiches in the plant's executive cafeteria after the inspection, Crow gratified the manager by praising Tyson and Varney's good work, and by promising to take any of their concerns to the Prefect. The manager, beaming with relief at what he assumed to have been a narrow escape, was inclined to be chatty.

"It's good that the Exarch sent you to Northwind," he said, "and not somebody else."

Crow wondered if the manager would think the same thing if he knew that the Paladin sitting across the table from him was only there because he needed to avoid Tara Campbell until he could figure out whether he wanted to move closer or to run away. "Is it really?"

"Yeah," said the plant manager. "I wasn't born yesterday; I know that Paladins are only human. We could have gotten handed over to somebody who was more interested in pulling rank on the locals than in working with them—and that would have been a disaster, especially last summer. But you and the Prefect worked together like you'd been on the same team since preschool."

Somewhat to Crow's surprise, the offhand remark did much to clarify his own conflicted feelings. He had been thinking of Tara Campbell as a hostage to fortune, and—as the manager had just unwittingly pointed out—such an estimate was seriously in error. She was a power in her own right, a leader whose strength and skills complemented his. Any closeness between the two of them would only serve to lighten his burden, not to make it greater. Together, they would truly become a force to be reckoned with.

He thanked the plant manager for his kind words and made his farewells, then headed back toward the capital city and the New Barracks feeling considerably happier than he had upon awaking. He was not a man given to public displays of emotion, but inwardly, at least, he was smiling as he made his way up the stairs to his quarters. He would wash away the grime of today's travel, he thought, and put on new clothes. Then he would go speak again with Tara Campbell.

There was a fat envelope lying on the dining table in his quarters when he entered. The sight gave him pause for a moment—the envelope had not been there when he left. The exterior had his name and rank written on it in black marker, with a scrawl of different-colored ink showing that Security down at the main door had signed for the delivery in his absence. Security would have passed the envelope along to the regular cleaning crew when they came in to clean the floors and change the bed linen and wash his plates and teacups.

He opened the envelope, only to find another envelope inside. This one bore a different address:

LIEUTENANT JUNIOR GRADE DANIEL PETERSON
CHANG-AN
LIAO

"No," he said. "No."

Letting the inner envelope fall unopened from suddenly nerveless fingers, he sank into the chair and buried his face in his hands.

27

Jasmine Flower Wine Shop
Chang-An
Liao, Prefecture V
October 3111; local summer

He sat at a table in the corner back with his head in his hands. A bottle, not the first of the evening, stood at his elbow; and next to the bottle, a wineglass. He was trying his best to drink himself into oblivion, and oblivion was not cooperating.

The Jasmine Flower Wine Shop was on the outskirts of Chang-An—far away from the current fighting, and even farther away from the burnt-out shell of the urban center. Any resistance going on inside the city came from desperate civilians. The local military units had been crushed during the first days of the fighting, wiped out as an effective force for the crime of daring to resist when the Capellan Confederation landed a DropShip and started disembarking soldiers.

The CapCons had double-berthed—maybe even triple-berthed—their DropShip. They'd packed it with two or three times the number of soldiers it should have carried; they'd overstuffed its cargo holds with armored vehicles, with heavy weapons, and with BattleMechs. A single DropShip of that class was not rated to carry so much; it should not have been able to carry more than the local defenses in Chang-An could have dealt with handily.

He had worked the numbers out carefully—he was good at such exercises—before he had even considered . . . but he had not considered that the Capellans would lie, or that they would put a DropShip at such risk.

That was the first betrayal.

No, he thought. Be honest with yourself, at least. It was the second.

He poured himself another glass of wine. His hands were shaking so that he had to steady the neck of the bottle against the lip of the glass. He managed to still the trembling long enough to pick up the wineglass and drain it without spilling. The wine was a heavy red from the dry temperate coast, harsh and tannic; his head was full of its fumes. They didn't help to get the smell of burning out of his nostrils, or out of his memories.

Chang-An's public health services had dug common graves for the city's innumerable dead—drivers of earthmovers and IndustrialMechs risking their lives to furrow up ground out of the way of the fighting, then laying the bodies out in rows like seed for an obscene crop someday to come. He had brought his parents' bodies there himself and put them in; they had no other friends or family left alive to do it. And the earthmovers had covered them up again.

That had been the first night he'd tried to get drunk. But he hadn't been able to get drunk enough.

Three more DropShips had come down at the port today; more soldiers poured out of them into the city and the surrounding countryside. He had seen them, had gone back and hidden in the shadows to watch. He'd seen transport aircraft, too, and heavy gear— Saxon APCs, Maxim Mk2 Transports, even a Mobile Tactical Command HQ—all of it meant for supporting large-scale field maneuvers, not for city fighting.

And this wasn't the equipment for a quick raid. It was take-the-whole-planet stuff. He knew the theory; he had studied it, and had been at the top of his class. He had never seen the theory at work until now.

Another betrayal, that.

One ship, and one ship only; that had been the word. He knew distances, and he knew the times to and from the jump points. There was no way additional ships could have come this quickly, even in response to a maximum-priority HPG message. The new ships had to have started on their way before the first ship had even landed.

He buried his face in his hands again. The Cap-Cons had lied to him from the beginning, and he had believed their lies. There was not enough wine in

Chang-An to make that better. Maybe not enough wine on all of Liao.

The table shifted under his elbows, and the bench opposite him creaked as somebody sat down uninvited. Unwillingly, he lifted his head, and saw a slender, smiling, ordinary-featured man in a CapCon uniform. The last time he'd seen him, the man had worn civilian clothing.

"You're a very difficult young man to find these days, Lieutenant Peterson."

"Go away."

"Now, now. Is that any way to speak to your benefactor?"

"I have a benefactor? I don't see anyone like that in here." He gave a harsh, choking laugh. "Just a traitor and a lying bastard. Respectively."

The CapCon shook his head, still smiling. "A bit late for second thoughts, I'm afraid. The thing is done."

He said nothing, willing the man to go away. A useless effort—the smiling man only crooked his finger at the wineshop waiter for another glass. When it arrived, he filled it, unbidden, and sipped, shuddering.

"Dreadful stuff, this. You could do better with us."

"I don't think so."

"We brought our own vintages—the better to toast your name after the first landing."

The sudden flash of anger cut like a knife through the dullness of despair. "You promised me that my name would never be spoken."

Smiling, still smiling, the man said, "And it was not. We drank our toasts to the Betrayer of Liao."

"Get out."

"All in good time. I came here with a purpose, you know."

"If I let you tell me about it, will you leave?" He made a disgusted sound deep in his throat. "Go ahead."

The man reached into the pocket of his uniform tunic and pulled out a card with a name, a rank, and an address printed on one side, and a string of numbers neatly handwritten on the other.

"This is the number for your account on Terra. The agreed-upon funds are there and waiting for you to access them." He laid the card down on the tabletop next to the wineglass and rose to leave. "As is a bonus of one stone for each Republic citizen killed in the fighting. You see, we are not ungrateful."

And the smiling man was gone.

He waited, trembling with rage, but the smiling man did not come back. The anger built and built. At length he got to his feet, moving slowly and deliberately. He was holding so much anger, he thought, that moving too fast might break him. He wrapped his fingers carefully around the neck of the empty wine bottle.

"Toasted my name." He spoke to himself in a steadily rising whisper. "My name. *My name.*"

He lifted the bottle and threw it against the back wall of the wineshop so hard that it shattered. A few seconds later, the wineglass followed it.

"Not any more."

The wineshop waiter was staring at him, and he knew it was time to leave—leave the shop, leave the city, leave the world. Daniel Peterson had died on the first day of the fighting in Chang-An. When he figured out who he was now, he'd give himself another name.

He almost left the smiling man's business card behind on the table. In the end, though, he picked up the card and took it with him. Because it didn't matter who he was going to become.

He'd always need the money.

= 28 =

South of Benderville
Oilfields Coast
Northwind
February 3134; dry season

By noon, the cockpit of Brigadier General Michael Griffin's *Koshi* was hotter than a steam bath. Despite the best efforts of generations of designers, the 'Mech had not yet been built that didn't leave its pilot sweating like a pig. Griffin had been drinking water steadily since early morning, along with extra rations of the specially formulated drinks issued to regular troopers during desert maneuvers, and to MechWarriors any time an extended stay in the 'Mech's cockpit was required.

It was nevertheless a good thing, Griffin thought,

that he wasn't planning on a brisk bout of hand-to-hand combat any time soon. He knew from experience that after marching the *Koshi* with the task force all day long, he would leave the cockpit at nightfall feeling—as his grandmother would have said—like he'd been beaten all over with a broom handle.

At least the polarized ferroglass viewports cut out the worst of the glare bouncing off the miles and miles of water and sand that passed for scenery along the Oilfields Coast. The soldiers outside would need protective goggles, which some of them would not wear because of the discomfort or because of the reduction in their field of view, and heavy-duty sunscreen, which some of them would, inevitably, forget. At nightfall, both groups would complain of eyestrain and sunburn, and would rest poorly. Then the next day, it would all begin again—and still they had found no sign of Anastasia Kerensky.

A fruitless search under uncomfortable conditions, Griffin thought, wasn't going to do any good for morale. But orders were orders, and there was nothing to do but go on.

The radio in the 'Mech's cockpit crackled. A moment later, a voice came through on one of the secure channels.

"Command, this is Balac Two."

"Go ahead, Balac Two," Griffin replied.

"I have an aircraft on visual."

Griffin felt a stirring of excitement. Were the task force's long hours of heat and discomfort finally about to pay off? A man could always hope.

"Do you have an ID on the aircraft?" he asked.

"I make it a Donar Assault Helicopter."

The Donar was a known Steel Wolf unit. Even better, the identification matched with the aircraft the boy had described the night before. *Thank you, youngster,* Griffin thought. *I think we've got a hit.*

Aloud, he said, "Good work, Balac Two. Have you been spotted?"

"I don't think so. Looks like he's doing a routine patrol."

"Any sight of something that might be a DropShip?"

"That's a negative. No DropShips."

"The Wolf has to have come from somewhere. Stick with him, Balac Two; see if you can follow him home."

"Yes, sir. Balac Two out."

Brigadier General Michael Griffin was happy. Outside the cockpit of the 'Mech, all he could see was deep blue water out to the horizon on his right hand, and grassy brown sand hills out to the horizon on his left, and the rutted dirt track that was the grandly named Kearney Coastal Highway stretching out ahead. But somewhere beyond all that, at last, lay the object of the past several days' tedious search—the hiding place of Anastasia Kerensky's DropShips.

He raised his aide-de-camp Lieutenant Jones on the command circuit. "Balac Two's spotted our Wolf."

"High time," said Jones. "Shall I put the troops on alert?"

"Continue reconnaissance here on the ground, but have them ready. There's no guarantee the Wolf won't come after Balac Two and bring his buddies with him."

Time passed. Griffin sweated, from tension as much as from the heat of the 'Mech's cockpit. The only thing moving within his field of vision that wasn't the Highlanders themselves was something four-legged and reptilian throwing up a flurry of sand off next to the road. Griffin, native to the Kearney coastline, recognized the signs of a scaley-bogle going after slower-moving prey.

Good for him, Griffin thought. He's going to eat tonight.

The radio crackled again. "Command, this is Balac One."

Balac One was the VTOL taking the seaward leg today, while Balac Two did the landward search. "Go ahead, Balac One."

"I have Balfour-Douglas Petrochemicals Offshore Drilling Station Number Forty-seven on the horizon."

"Any sight of the DropShips, Balac One?"

"Negative, sir. No DropShips in sight."

"Give Balfour-Douglas a flyover, see if you can raise them. Maybe they've noticed something that we haven't."

"Yes, sir. Heading toward Balfour-Douglas now—wait a minute. Sir, I have Balac Two and the Wolf both on visual, heading this way."

Quickly, Griffin opened a second circuit. "Balac Two, this is Command. Have you been spotted?"

"Negative. Looks like our buddy's in a hurry to get home."

Griffin frowned. The Wolf was heading out to sea, toward Balac One and away from the landward-searching Balac Two. Not the direction he'd have ex-

pected for a VTOL returning to base, not unless—
"Damn," he said under his breath, and keyed both
of the secure circuits back open.

"Balac One, Balac Two—he'll be heading for the
VTOL pad on that Balfour-Douglas rig. Shadow
him—don't let him spot you—see what's up out
there and report back to me."

Anastasia Kerensky's on-planet field headquarters,
close enough to be vulnerable to a quick strike out
of Fort Barrett—General Griffin was already juggling
troop numbers and battle scenarios in his head as he
made ready to pass the word along to his aide.

We haven't yet found the DropShips, he thought
happily, but maybe we've found the next best thing.

29

Balfour-Douglas Petrochemicals Offshore Drilling
Station #47
Oilfields Coast
Northwind
February 3134; dry season

Ian Murchison stood looking out across the water
toward the Kearney coast. It wasn't his usual hour
for spending time on #47's observation deck—bright
noon, with sunlight dazzling off blue water and a
breeze blowing off the land, and the scavenging sea-
birds wheeling and calling overhead—but this was
not, even in his current circumstances, one of his
usual days.

The strangeness had begun with a summons from
Galaxy Commander Anastasia Kerensky, bringing

him post-haste from sickbay up to her quarters, where the body of Star Colonel Nicholas Darwin lay sprawled across the wide bed in a welter of blood. Anastasia Kerensky stood nearby, a silent presence in black leather.

Murchison checked the body for breathing and pulse, and found neither. Darwin's throat had been cut brutally and efficiently, with his arms trapped in his clothing to give him no chance for resistance. "He's past anything I can do for him."

Anastasia said, "That was the general idea."

"What happened?"

"You were right."

He suppressed the urge to say that he was sorry. The Galaxy Commander had the look, at the moment, of someone who would kill the first person who expressed sympathy. Instead, he asked, "What do you need me to do, then?"

"Help me get him outside and up to the observation deck. I want to make it crystal-clear what happens to people who think they can sell out the Steel Wolves."

Why me? Murchison wanted to ask, but he knew better.

He had already figured out that his relationship with Anastasia Kerensky, as her personal Bondsman, possessed levels of complexity that—as one not raised in the Clan culture—he could not truly understand. This was apparently one of those levels. Beyond that, however, he had pointed Anastasia's suspicions in Nicholas Darwin's way to start with; and he could not help but feel that the act made him, in some way, complicit in Darwin's death. It was fitting, therefore, that he be involved in the sticky aftermath.

He considered the technical aspects of the problem. At least no one was trying to hide the body . . . "The easiest way is probably to roll him up in the bedsheets and carry him out between us. Those sheets are going to be a write-off anyhow. And the mattress."

"There are other beds to sleep in," she said curtly. "Wrap him up."

Together, they heaved the body and the sheets off the bed and rolled them up into an ugly bloodstained sausage of flesh and blood-soaked fabric. Murchison had pulled on a pair of latex examining gloves by habit when he first approached Darwin's body—he carried them in his belt pouch along with shears and a screwdriver, much as Kerensky and her Wolves habitually carried knives—but Anastasia worked barehanded. It made sense, he thought; there was already blood on her hands.

He took one end of the finished bundle, and Anastasia the other. In death, Darwin made a limp, ungainly weight. They didn't need to go far to get to the observation deck— down the corridor, down the cross-corridor, into the elevator, up and out—but it was too great a distance to cover unnoticed. They only encountered one person along the way, another from the general forgettable mass of Steel Wolf Warriors, who said nothing while watching them, avideyed—but by the time they emerged with their burden onto the observation platform, a small crowd already stood waiting.

Anastasia Kerensky was full of a magnificent disregard. Murchison, for his part, was grateful that nobody expected a Bondsman to explain anything. She let her end of the Darwin-bundle fall to the platform's surface with a muffled thud, and he lowered his a bit more gently.

"Rope," she said. "Or chain, it doesn't matter."

Murchison didn't ask questions. He went in search of rope and left Anastasia standing over Nicholas Darwin's sheet-wrapped body, with the wind off the land whipping her red-black hair back from her face like a bloodstained sable banner. More Warriors had gathered on the observation platform. Gossip moved as fast with the Steel Wolves as it did with anyone else, and by now every soul on the rig probably knew that something had happened.

Nobody said anything to Murchison. He was the Galaxy Commander's Bondsman, after all, and what he did was her business and not theirs.

He found the rope—a coil of nylon line hanging from a hook next to one of the emergency lifesaving stations—and brought it back to Anastasia. As he came up to her, she bent down, grabbed the edge of the sheet in both hands and jerked. Darwin's body rolled out onto the deck.

"Tie it around his feet," she said.

Her voice wasn't particularly loud, but it rang out in the silence like a bell. The Steel Wolves on the observation deck weren't watching or listening to anything else but her, and she was paying them no attention at all. Murchison squatted down next to the body and worked with the nylon line until he had a snug loop fitted around Darwin's ankles. He stood up again and waited, holding the coil of line in his hand.

Anastasia said, "Make the other end fast to the rail."

Her voice never changed, her face remained an impassive mask, and there was blood drying red and sticky on her hands. Murchison was torn between cold-to-the-bone fear of her very presence and a reluctant admiration. God only knew, he thought, what her Wolves felt at the sight of her.

He tied the other end of the line to the top bar of the safety railing that surrounded the observation platform, and stepped back.

"Good," she said. She stooped then, knees bent, and took Darwin's body under the armpits. "Get his feet."

Murchison obeyed. He didn't need to be told anything further—they both rose, lifting Darwin's body up with them, and the change of direction in her gaze was enough. They held Darwin between them, raised him shoulder-high to clear the railing, and threw him over. The line paid out, whistling, and snapped taut.

"No one sells out the Wolves and lives to spend the money they got for it," said Anastasia Kerensky. "*No one.*"

She stood at the rail, her back to her assembled Warriors, staring fixedly out to sea and gripping the rail in her bloodstained hands. There was a long silence. The Warriors were waiting for her order to disperse, and she wasn't saying anything.

Then Murchison saw her eyes widen. She was looking at something now, not gazing blankly out at the landward horizon. He followed her gaze.

A dot. No, two dots, moving rapidly and growing larger, one of them following the other. Aircraft.

Anastasia Kerensky spoke. Her voice had a different tone to it now, the snap of action rather than the measured beat of judgment. "How many birds do we have up on patrol? Anybody?"

"One, Galaxy Commander," a voice replied out of the watching crowd.

"Then we have been found. Pass the word to the VTOL pilot: Weapons free, eliminate pursuit if possible." She swung away from the railing to face the assembled Wolves. "For a little while, we still have the element of surprise. Prepare to lift the DropShips and attack."

30

South of Benderville
Oilfields Coast
Northwind
February 3134; dry season

Brigadier General Griffin's task force continued southward in the reported direction of the Steel Wolf VTOL. The day continued eerily quiet, with nothing to look at but the sea and the grassy sand hills and the cloud of dust thrown up by the reconnaissance column. Despite the apparent calm, Griffin's muscles were tight with worry and the need for action. He wanted to be fighting something, releasing his tension by putting the *Koshi* through moves designed to cause death and destruction, rather than continuing his steady pace forward while he listened to the running reports from Balacs One and Two.

"Command, this is Balac One. Our Wolf is definitely making for that oil rig. Balac Two is on his tail."

Griffin keyed on the circuit. "Balac One, this is Command. Does the Wolf know Balac Two is on him?"

"That appears to be a negative . . . no. Damn. He's putting on speed."

"Command, this is Balac One. I've been spotted."

"Stay with him, Balac One," Griffin ordered. Thoughts passed through his head in a rush. There was a slim chance that the unidentified VTOL belonged to Balfour-Douglas—coming back from a supply run, maybe, or responding to a medical emergency—and that this was a false alarm. "Hail him and request identification."

Even as he gave the order, he admitted to himself that he didn't believe in the VTOL's innocence. But learning that Anastasia Kerensky had possession of an offshore oil rig still wouldn't give him an answer to the main question—where in hell were the Steel Wolves hiding their DropShips?

He raised his aide-de-camp, Lieutenant Jones, on the command circuit. "Owain."

"Sir?"

"Send a message to the CO back at Fort Barrett: 'Possible enemy base sighted. Recommend you put all local forces on high alert.' Put my name and codes on it; you know the drill."

"Yes, sir."

There. That was covered. Griffin went back to waiting and listening. The sweat that ran down his back and shoulders was not all from sitting in a 'Mech's cockpit in the noonday heat.

The radio crackled. "Command, this is Balac One. The Wolf is not responding to hails."

"Keep on him, Balac One. Balac Two, do you still have both units on visual?"

"That's affirmative," came the distant, tinny voice of the pilot of the second Balac. "The Wolf is still on course for the oil rig—no, wait, he's turning."

"Command, this is Balac One—the Wolf's doubling back on me. Permission to engage?"

"Permission granted, Balac One." Balacs mounted a single heavy machine gun and a pair of Advanced Tactical Missile three-packs. The armament loadout wasn't meant for prolonged engagements—Balacs were cavalry, not artillery, meant to strike hard and get out fast—but this encounter wasn't likely to be prolonged. "Balac Two, can you see what's going on?"

"Affirmative, sir. Balac One is firing—it's a clean miss—the Wolf is holding fire and maintaining course and speed toward Balac One—Balac One's firing again. The Wolf's hit!—but he's still coming, he's letting go with all his missiles at once, and Balac One's been hit . . . Balac One is down . . . Permission to close the distance and engage, sir?"

Balac Two sounded hungry for action, wanting it badly—the pilot of Balac One had probably been a friend. Griffin knew how he felt. The knowledge wasn't going to help.

"Permission denied, Balac Two—they have to know by now that we're on to them. Turn around and get back here as fast as you can."

"Yes, sir. Balac Two returning t—" The voice transmission ended in a burst of earsplitting cacophony.

"Balac Two?" Griffin tried the circuit again. "Balac Two?"

Nothing came through in response except the painful noise of fried or jammed comms. Resigned, already knowing in his heart what would happen, he tried first the command circuit—"Owain? Lieutenant Jones?"—and the general circuit, without success. "Damn."

At least everybody can see me, he thought, and raised the *Koshi*'s massive arm in the visual signal for the column to halt. Then, moving stiffly—it had been a long tense morning and the day wasn't over yet—he unstrapped from the cockpit's command seat, stashed the neurohelmet, and made his way out and down the exit ladder to the sandy ground outside.

The stiff breeze chilled him at the same time as it blew white sand against his sweat-slicked arms and torso, coating him with a fine layer of grit. Lieutenant Jones was already waiting for him with water—over a gallon of it, in a collapsible plastic jug. Griffin poured half of the tepid water over his head, neck, and arms, and began drinking the rest in long, thirsty swallows.

Jones said, "The bastards jammed us. Sir."

"I know," Griffin said, between pulls at the water jug. "At least it eliminates any doubt that these are the Wolves we're dealing with."

"Orders?"

"Keep the troops on alert, make ready to head back to Fort Barrett on my word. We don't have what it takes to winkle Anastasia Kerensky out of an off-shore hideout, but they do. And keep trying the comms; whatever trick the Wolves played isn't going to last forever."

After that, there was nothing to do for a while except drink more of the water and wait for Balac Two to make its appearance. Griffin knew that the column couldn't remain halted indefinitely. At some point—and this was what the Regiment paid people like him for—he would have to make the call, decide that Balac Two had joined Balac One in the deep water off the Oilfields Coast, and march back north leaving what remained of the Balacs and their pilots behind.

Thinking about it later—but not much later—Griffin realized that Balac Two had made good time on the return flight. He'd barely begun to consider the various worst-case scenarios before the VTOL came screaming down into a cloud-of-dust landing on the dirt road ahead of the recon column.

The Balac's cockpit opened and the pilot climbed out. General Griffin and Lieutenant Jones hurried to join him.

"Sir!" The pilot was panting—as much from nerves, Griffin judged, as from exertion. "Some sort of jamming burst—I couldn't get through—"

"We know, son," Griffin said. "All our comms are down hard as well. Any pursuit?"

"No, sir. I don't think the Wolf spotted me."

"Or he had other things on his mind." Griffin frowned. If I were Anastasia Kerensky, he thought, and I'd just figured out that my secret base wasn't so secret any more, what would I do? Put that way, it was easy. "She's going to move up the schedule for the main attack."

Lieutenant Jones was nodding. "It makes sense. But move it up to when?"

Griffin drew his breath to answer, but was stopped by an outcry from among the troops. He turned his head and saw one of the sergeants—Gordon, that was it, a big man, head and shoulders taller than most of his fellows—shouting and pointing out to sea.

Very quietly, at his shoulder, he heard Lieutenant Jones say, "Damn."

Out on the seaward horizon, the water was boiling. White froth churned the surface of the water so furiously that the naked eye could see the tumult from the shore, and great billowing clouds of steam ascended toward heaven. Then, slowly, rising up like Leviathan out of the deeps, came a great silver shape, shouldering the water aside and lifting itself upward as it pulled free of the ocean's grip . . . a DropShip.

And another, and another, and another, coming up from the water like bubbles and dwindling into the upper air.

And Griffin knew—because he would have done the same, if he had the Steel Wolves and their DropShips and, for a few hours only, the element of surprise—where it was that Anastasia Kerensky was going. "Owain."

"Sir." His aide-de-camp looked stunned. They all did; Griffin suspected that his own expression at the moment wasn't much more reassuring. It couldn't be helped; they had to act now and stop shaking later.

"Come with me. We're going to have to abandon

the *Koshi* until a tech can come out here from Fort Barrett with the start-up codes. I'm going on ahead in the Balac."

"Sir?"

"We're going to have to strip Fort Barrett naked, Lieutenant, and get a relief force ready to move out as soon as possible. Anastasia Kerensky isn't going to mess around with landing on the salt flats this time. She's going to be heading straight for the main DropPort—and with our comms down, nobody in Tara is going to know that she's coming."

=== 31 ===

New Barracks
Tara
Northwind
February 3134; local winter

Ezekiel Crow was still sitting at the dining table in his quarters. The bulky envelope with its deadly, betraying address lay unopened on the table by his elbow.

> LIEUTENANT JUNIOR GRADE DANIEL PETERSON
> CHANG-AN
> LIAO

He didn't know how long he had been sitting there, not moving, not even thinking—unless you could count the prison of unwilling memory as thought. But as he came back, slowly, to the present time and place, he saw that the sky outside the windows was dark now; there had been daylight left when he arrived home and found the envelope waiting for him.

He hadn't opened it yet. He had been afraid, when fear for his life was another thing he thought that he'd left behind in the ruins. But an envelope coming to him bearing that name and that address could not possibly contain anything good.

He had cut all ties to his former life when he changed his name and left Chang-An. He had never looked back. There shouldn't have been anything left in The Republic that could connect Ezekiel Crow, Paladin of the Sphere, with the infamous—and never found or identified—Betrayer of Liao.

Shouldn't have been, the voice of reason pointed out, doesn't mean that there wasn't. You might as well go ahead and look. There's no point in putting it off any longer.

Reluctantly, he opened the envelope and took out the contents. The first thing to meet his fingers was a sealed letter, which he set aside. He'd have plenty of time later to look at the blackmailer's bill. Besides the letter, the envelope contained documentation: photographs, medical records, copies of old files and old news stories, and a slim, paperbound book.

The last item puzzled him until he looked closer. It was nonfiction, a bit of autobiography from a publishing house with its headquarters in the Capellan Confederation. Based on the jacket copy, the author—now a popular novelist of some local fame in the

CapCon worlds—had been a minor intelligence officer during the Confederation-Republic conflicts of recent decades, including the period covering the Liao Massacre. Like many another old soldier, he had taken advantage of newly relaxed classification levels to revisit the wars of his youth.

The relevant section of the memoir proved easy to find. After all, Crow knew the sequence of events well. Yes, there it was: ". . . secured the cooperation, for a fee, of a disgruntled junior officer in the planetary militia, one Daniel Petersen, in allowing the initial DropShip landing. . . ."

A wave of strong irritation briefly washed out Crow's fear. I was *not* disgruntled. I had a plan.

A plan that didn't work.

It *should* have worked. The Republic had been ignoring CapCon terrorist activity on Liao for years—"too low-level to risk destabilizing the local situation," they said. A full-scale armed incursion would have been something they couldn't just shove into the closet and wish away. If the CapCons hadn't triple-loaded the initial DropShip, Liao's own defense forces could have held them at the port.

You took their money, said the voice of reason, and you didn't expect them to cheat? You *deserved* to have your plan blown to pieces on the first day.

Crow told the voices in his head to stop arguing. His old stupidity—and he agreed, he had been amazingly stupid when he was young—didn't matter anymore. The path leading to the fatal discovery was clear. His enemy, whoever that might be, had chanced to read this book, and had caught the passing reference to Daniel Peterson—and had pulled on that single thread until the whole fabric unraveled.

He felt a strong urge to destroy the contents of the envelope, but he knew that it would do no good. The items sent to him would all be copies or duplicates; the originals would be kept safely elsewhere.

Instead, he forced himself to think about the problem as objectively as possible. How bad was it, really? Allegations—it was always wise to think in terms of allegations rather than facts—could be countered, threats could be neutralized, but not from here on Northwind. For that, he needed access to the Senate and to the Exarch and to the influential media; in short, he needed to be on Terra.

I have to leave here now, he thought. It shouldn't take much more than a couple of months to handle this, as long as I'm in the right place. And as soon as I've taken care of everything, I can come back.

Actually getting to Terra, however, presented difficulties. He needed a DropShip, and preferably a civilian DropShip. Was there one in port? He tried to remember the schedule for the shipping line that had won the mail-service contract for Prefecture III in the aftermath of the HPG disaster, and realized that he couldn't remember it, or even the name of the shipping line itself. Stupid, he thought. You've been slipping, and you never noticed.

He'd also put off the inevitable for too long already. Willing his hands to steadiness, he opened the sealed letter.

It wasn't handwritten. Not surprising; he might have recognized the handwriting of a known enemy or a supposed friend. Anonymous black words printed out on white paper could have come from anyone. The paper itself was of high quality, but that meant nothing. Anyone who could afford to track down Daniel Peterson—a person who had, in all but the crudest physical sense, died twenty-three years ago in Chang-An, his identity put into a mass grave with all the rest of the dead and covered up with dirt—anyone with that much money could afford to use good paper for his or her blackmail notes.

The letter contained only three sentences:

> Farrell's mercenaries are at your disposal. Anastasia Kerensky wants Northwind. See that she gets what she wants.

32

The New Barracks
Tara
Northwind
February 3134; local winter

Captain Tara Bishop was working late in her office at the New Barracks. Night had already fallen outside, but she still had files and papers to go through in the interest of preparing economic and intelligence summaries for the Prefect—who had left her own office and gone back to her quarters precisely at the end of the working day, in direct contravention of her usual practice. Tara Campbell was a habitual overstayer at the office, to Captain Bishop's periodic dismay—since unlike the Prefect, the Captain had something approaching a private social life.

Of course, the Captain thought, there was always the chance that Tara Campbell had at last acquired a social life of her own that didn't revolve around will-attend, will-have-fun diplomatic and military occasions. The Prefect hadn't said anything to that effect—she was a very private person, most likely in response to having grown up in the political spotlight—but she'd had the look about her this morning. Not as tense as usual, and happier, and just a little smug. Captain Bishop recognized the signs, and there was only one person who could be the cause.

I wonder, Bishop thought, if I tracked down our friend Paladin Crow, would he be smug and happy too?

Captain Bishop smiled to herself and opened up the next file. She wasn't going to begrudge either one of them the chance. Both the Prefect and the Paladin were too straight-arrow to let a relationship get in the way of their duty; what would have been hormone-addled slacking off in less driven and committed types was likely to manifest itself in the pair of them as nothing more than a retreat from their usual high levels of overwork.

And even that, she suspected, wouldn't last for long. Give them a while to get used to the idea, and they'd go right back to working eighteen-hour days. They'd just be working them together instead of separately.

Captain Bishop turned her attention to an economic report on reforestation policies in the planet's lumber-producing regions. She was scarcely a page in, and chewing her way through a dense paragraph on the development of second-growth forests in the lower Rockspires, when her desk's communications console suddenly erupted in flashing red lights and began sounding an alarm. And not her own desk alone—the sound-and-light display was also coming from the Prefect's empty desk in the outer office, with backup alarms echoing from desks both occupied and unoccupied all over this part of the building.

. The alert might be sounding throughout the New Barracks, but the message was coming in straight to the Prefect's desk. Captain Bishop pushed the button that routed the absent Prefect's calls to her own desk, picked up the handset, and said, "Prefect's office Captain Bishop speaking this is not a secure line how may I help you?" all in one rapid nonstop breath.

"This is Tara DropPort," said the voice on the other end of the line. "We have DropShips landing without authorization. I say again, DropShips landing without authorization."

Oh damn, Captain Bishop thought. Oh damn oh damn oh damn. We didn't find them in time.

With her free hand, she slapped the button that sent the "wake up and get the hell back up here" alarm to the Prefect's quarters. As an afterthought, she sent it to the Paladin's as well, then went on to hit the General Quarters alarm, the signal that would have every soldier in the New Barracks at his or her duty station within minutes.

At same time, she asked, "Do you have an ID on the ships, DropPort?"

"It's the Steel Wolves—we saw their insignia and configuration enough times last summer to know."

"Recommend you evacuate your personnel now, DropPort."

"Already on it," said the voice at the other end. "It'll take the Wolves a little while to open up and roll on out, and everybody who isn't going to fight should be gone by then. We've got a couple of civilian ships caught down on the ground; they'll just have to button up tight and wait for the dust to settle."

The DropPort commander sounded calm, almost cheerful, but Captain Bishop knew it for the calm that comes after ceasing to waste energy on things like hope. If the Wolves were planning to force their way from the landing field into Tara proper, the fighting was going to be vicious, and the troops stationed at the DropPort would be the city's first line of defense. Bishop racked her brains, trying to remember the size of the force stationed at the port. Her mind eventually supplied her with a dismayingly small number.

This, she thought, is going to be a very long night.

Even the few minutes it took for the Prefect to come at a run from her quarters to the office in the New Barracks seemed to stretch out forever. When the Prefect arrived, Captain Bishop handed over the conversation with the DropPort commander—and the responsibility for the defense of the entire planet—with an unvoiced sigh of relief. Ezekiel Crow arrived a few minutes later, looking grim.

"Paladin Crow," the Prefect said as soon as he entered the office, "I need you to take command of Farrell's mercenaries. If we can hit the Wolves from two directions at once before they penetrate too deep into the city, we've got a good chance at pushing them back onto their ships. Or at least of pinning them down hard enough to force a negotiation."

"Anastasia Kerensky doesn't negotiate, that I've noticed," Crow said.

"Then she needs to learn," said Tara Campbell. "And I'm counting on you to help me teach her."

=== 33 ===

The Balac Strike VTOL taking the General back to Fort Barrett took off in a cloud of white dust and arrowed away northward at top speed. Will Elliot was already urging the members of his scout/sniper platoon back onto their Shandras before the noise of its departure died. Up and down the line he could hear the voices of Jock and Lexa and the other sergeants chivvying the rest of the soldiers into the troop trucks. Not more than a minute later, the major who commanded the reinforced rifle company—with

General Griffin gone he'd be the senior officer, and in command of the whole task force—gave the order to mount up and move out.

"Sarge?"

That voice, on the other hand, belonged to one of the privates in the scout/sniper platoon. Will suppressed the urge to look over his shoulder for Master Sergeant Murray or Sergeant Donahue or one of the other godlike figures of his own early enlistment.

"What is it, soldier?" he asked.

"Were those the DropShips we've been looking for?"

Will bit his tongue. Be patient, he thought. You were this green once yourself, not so long ago. "That's right, soldier."

"Where do you think they've gone?"

"I don't think anything," Will said. "But the General thinks they're heading for Tara."

"What about us, Sarge?"

That one was easy. "We're going back to Fort Barrett, on the double. And after that, we're going where we're told."

Thinking on it afterward, Will decided that the forced march back to Fort Barrett rated as one of the most unpleasant experiences of his entire first term of enlistment—worse even than making a fighting retreat out of Red Ledge Pass in the pouring rain. The misery that time hadn't lasted nearly as long, and he'd been able to relieve his feelings by shooting at things. This was nothing but hard going from before dawn to after dark, in the choking dust and the relentless sun. The column stopped periodically for rest and food, but only long enough to ensure that the soldiers did not collapse from exhaustion. But worst of all was knowing that on the other side of the world, the Steel Wolves had already landed at Tara DropPort.

When the column arrived at Fort Barrett, they found the base in a state of furious activity. The barracks were crowded with soldiers from units normally stationed at smaller bases all over Kearney; some units were even housed in rows of tents set up on the sports field and the parade ground. And every Regimental troop-transport aircraft in Kearney—or what looked like it—was lined up on the landing field, wingtip to wingtip, with barely enough room left open for landing and takeoff. Mixed in among them were passenger craft bearing the insignia of three different civilian airlines.

Lexa McIntosh whistled in amazement as soon as she saw the civilian aircraft. "Where the hell did they get those?"

"The General commandeered them, I suppose," Will said.

"Can he do that?"

Jock said, "Doesn't look like anybody's stopping him."

"I'm surprised he hasn't sent troops off to Tara already," Lexa said. "I don't know what the Wolves are planning, but it can't be good."

"They have to be bleeding over there," Jock rumbled in agreement.

Will shook his head. "Look at it. He's planning to hit the Steel Wolves with everything that Kearney's got." He was speaking slowly, because he hadn't had to think about things this way before. "It must have taken him this long to get all those aircraft together, and to get all the troops and supplies and weapons ready."

"Couldn't he have sent some on ahead?" Lexa wondered.

"He probably wishes he could send *himself* on ahead," Will said. "Remember the Pass—he was in the thick of it there. But he can't do any good this time unless he brings enough muscle with him to make a difference."

34

Ezekiel Crow left the New Barracks at a run, heading for the hangars outside the Armory where the 'Mechs were stored. The Countess of Northwind's words rang in his head:

Take command of Farrell's mercenaries. If we can hit the Wolves from two directions at once before they get too deep into the city, we've got a good chance at pushing them back onto their ships.

The Countess was right, he thought. Bringing the mercenaries into action was the solution to the current problem. The regimental forces in and around

Tara would not be enough by themselves to meet the attack. Anastasia Kerensky would have brought more Wolves to the battle this time than she had before—all of the ones who hadn't gone home to Tigress, augmented by those who had left Tigress over the past months for an unknown destination. The Highlanders needed the mercenaries to make up their missing numbers, if the streets of Tara were not going to become another Chang-An.

He could still stop it, Crow thought; he could . . . but other words also echoed in his mind, words not spoken but printed in cold black type on a sheet of good white paper:

Anastasia Kerensky wants Northwind. See that
she gets what she wants.

The letter contained no threat; whoever had written it hadn't seen the need. The information alone was enough to convey the desired message:

Keep Anastasia Kerensky from taking Northwind, and all of this becomes known.

When he reached the Armory he found it brightly lit despite the late hour, its windows and skylights glowing yellow against the dark. The whole building was full of furious activity, roused to action by the word from the port. Crow made for the 'Mech hangars, mostly empty until recent months, now filled with modified Industrial and Forestry and MiningMechs. There were only three real BattleMechs in the lot—Captain Bishop's *Pack Hunter*, the Countess's

Hatchetman, and Crow's own *Blade*. Not much, against the forces the Wolves would bring to bear.

The mercenaries would have more, he thought, and called the roll of them in his mind: a *Spider*, a *Firestarter*, a *Mad Cat III*, and Farrell's own *Jupiter*.

Those would be enough, if they were used.

His *Blade* waited in its hangar. To the guard outside, he said: "Paladin Crow, on the Prefect's business. I'm taking the 'Mech."

The *Blade* was probably his fastest way to the mercenaries, no matter what he decided to say when he got there. Ordinary vehicles—even tanks and armored cars—might be stopped and questioned, blocked and delayed. But nobody would force a 'Mech to halt; and even if somebody were foolish enough to try, Crow's *Blade* would be recognized, and people would assume he was on business too important to be stopped.

He climbed into the cockpit and dogged the hatch shut behind him. While the 'Mech's fusion engines and musculature were warming up, he quickly stripped down to his shorts, donned the cooling vest and neurohelmet, and slipped into the command chair. As soon as he'd gone through the primary and secondary security protocols needed to gain full access to the 'Mech's controls and capabilities, he switched the viewscreen over to IR mode. He'd need the infrared for taking the *Blade* through the city streets in the dark, and the cockpit's polarizing windows would mitigate the risk of getting blinded by flares and searchlights.

Another touch of the controls awakened the *Blade*'s fusion engine to full life. Crow brought the 'Mech out of the hangar, taking it past the New Barracks and past the Fort, into the streets of Tara. Soon the *Blade* was striding down the main road leading out of the city into the countryside beyond. Farrell's mercenary units had not yet been dispersed to garrison duty, but were still in their holding encampment; at the *Blade*'s cruising speed of seventy-six kilometers per hour, it would not take Crow long to reach them.

Then he would have to decide what he was going to do.

Giving over Tara—the city and Countess blurred together in his mind, until he wasn't certain which would be the more poignant loss—giving over Tara to the Steel Wolves would mean betrayal and bloody slaughter.

It's not as if you aren't used to it already, said the voice of reason, cold as always in the back of his head. Anastasia Kerensky wants Northwind, and the person who sent you that packet of damnation wants for you to give it to her—or have Paladin Ezekiel Crow unmasked to The Republic of the Sphere as the Betrayer of Liao.

How is that going to be different, he asked the voice of reason, from having him branded as the Betrayer of Northwind? Either way it brings me down. Is that the true goal—are Anastasia Kerensky and Countess Tara Campbell both nothing but pawns in somebody else's game to checkmate me?

The idea was not impossible. He'd said enough and done enough over the years that anyone involved in the upper levels of The Republic's politics could guess that he aimed high. And no one could rise to join the ranks of the Paladins, from whom the next Exarch would be chosen, without making enemies.

The line of thought brought a surge of irritation along with it. Later, he told himself, later he could sort out who had the whip hand over him, and why. But not now, not when the Steel Wolves were landing at the port and—*Farrell's mercenaries are at your disposal*—what Paladin Ezekiel Crow said and did in the next few hours would decide the course of the battle to come.

> Anastasia Kerensky wants Northwind. See that she gets what she wants.

There was something not quite right about that. Why should Anastasia Kerensky want Northwind, other than for the usual motives ascribed to the Clans: glory and reputation and a famous name? Why should she make a try—twice—for Northwind, instead of concentrating her attentions on places like Small World and Addicks? The Countess of Northwind had gotten it right, months ago when The Republic of the Sphere first sent him to Prefecture III: Northwind was the gateway to Terra.

Kerensky doesn't want Northwind, he thought. Kerensky wants Terra, just as the Clans have always wanted it. Seizing control of humanity's home planet would allow her to fulfill what the Clans believed to be their manifest destiny, and it would make her— what was the word they used?—*ilKhan*. Northwind was just the springboard.

The idea made sense, and chilled him even in the heat of the *Blade*'s cockpit. After Anastasia Kerensky had finished with Northwind, when the Highlanders' homeworld was no longer a threat at her back, then she would strike at Terra.

He'd reached the gates of the mercenary encampment while pursuing these thoughts, and was stopped by soldiers on gate guard with Gauss rifles, backed up by an SM1 Tank Destroyer.

"Halt and identify yourself, MechWarrior!"

A ceremonial threat, given muscle by the SM1. Crow replied over the *Blade*'s external speaker: "Paladin Ezekiel Crow. I need to speak with your commanding officer. At once."

From the *Blade*'s cockpit, he saw the gate guards put their heads together for a quick consultation. He didn't wait, but began unstrapping from the control seat and getting ready to climb down. The gate guards would have recognized Crow's name by now as that of the person who held the mercenaries' current contract. If Farrell were not already waiting by the time Crow reached the ground, he would be arriving in haste soon after.

In fact, Farrell showed up at the gate as Crow was stepping off the bottom rung of the access ladder. "Paladin Crow," he said. "To what do I owe this unexpected visit?"

"The Steel Wolves have landed at Tara DropPort."

"Huh." Farrell didn't look particularly surprised. "You're the one that's giving the orders, Paladin. What's the word?"

Crow, looking at Farrell, realized that the man didn't care what answer he got. At Crow's order, he would fight for the Northwinders, or against them, with equal skill and determination. His loyalty—if such was the word—was not to the cause, but to the contract, and to the man holding it.

The moment between Farrell's question and Crow's reply stretched out into infinity, with time within it for a host of considerations.

If I stay here and fight, he thought, it'll mean the end of my career. I might as well be dead for any use I'll be to The Republic after what's in that envelope gets published.

As for the Countess of Northwind—Crow realized with a pang of regret that whatever future they might have shared was lost to him, no matter what happened. Tara Campbell would never forgive the Betrayer of Liao.

On the other hand, the cold voice of reason pointed out, even without the aid of Jack Farrell's mercenaries, she would be able to hold out against the Steel Wolves for some time before having to admit defeat. Not forever—but long enough for Crow to reach Terra.

From Terra, he would have access to the resources that would let him deal with the threat of exposure as Daniel Peterson, Betrayer of Liao. The name was the connection, the only loose thread that could be pulled. If he could discredit or eliminate the source of the name, the rest would be nothing but rumor.

More than that, however—on Terra, he could protect The Republic of the Sphere and Devlin Stone's peace against the threat of invasion by the Steel Wolves. Such protection was the Exarch's responsibility, some people might say, but a crisis was no time for false modesty. If Damien Redburn was good at his job, Ezekiel Crow knew that he would be better.

"Take your forces," he said to Farrell. "Deploy them to block the roads out of the city. Don't give the Highlanders a chance to break off from combat and retreat."

"Do you want us to fight them," Farrell asked "or just to get in their way?"

"If you have to—fight."

PART THREE

Burning
February 3134

35

DropShip **Quicksilver**
Tara DropPort
Northwind
February 3134; local winter

By the time Ezekiel Crow had brought his *Blade* from
the mercenaries' encampment back to the city, the
hour was well past midnight. The city lay in eerie
quiet around him. The Wolves would have disem-
barked from their DropShips by now, and the port
complex itself had undoubtedly fallen; now they
would be moving cautiously forward, testing the defenses that Prefect Tara Campbell would have begun
setting up as soon as the DropPort sounded the
alarm. The Highlanders, for their part, were waiting
for Farrell's mercenaries to move into position before

starting their counterattack. They had a long wait ahead of them, Crow thought, and disappointment at the end of it.

He took his *Blade* through the streets leading to the DropPort. He had nothing else with him of his own except his MechWarrior's gear and the uniform—now stowed in the cockpit locker—which he had been wearing when he left the New Barracks for the Armory. The wallet containing his keys and ID and financial-access cards had still been in the pocket of his uniform trousers when the initial alarm sounded, which in retrospect was a good thing. He would not have liked to attempt a journey from Northwind to Terra backed by nothing but his personal charisma.

He would rather not have been making the journey at all. Running away, leaving a city to its fate . . . *I'm making a career of this,* he thought.

He shook his head. He was a Paladin of the Sphere. His loyalty was not to one world any longer, but to all of them, and to Terra above the rest. He had to go where he could to deal with the forces that threatened to stain his reputation, and where he could most effectively counter the threat of Anastasia Kerensky and her Steel Wolves.

Near morning, he reached the last checkpoint before the port: a barrier of wood and barbed wire, manned by combat troops in powered armor with a revetted gun emplacement and a comm set. Crow switched on the *Blade*'s external speakers.

"Paladin Crow, on Republic business," he said to the troopers.

He'd been able, by means of judicious detours, to avoid alerting any of the secondary checkpoints further in. This one, marking as it did a point in the Highlanders' outer defensive perimeter, could not as easily be circumvented, and he had already made up his mind not to try. The troopers here might send word back that Paladin Ezekiel Crow had passed through the lines in the direction of the port—but, with luck, not until it was too late for anyone to stop him.

The guards saluted him with their Gauss rifles and stepped back, raising the barrier. His *Blade* could have stepped over it without any difficulty, but to do so would have raised the alarm. Better to follow protocol, and buy himself time with polite behavior.

He continued on toward the DropPort. When the sound of gunfire marked the direction in which the Steel Wolves were making their first attempt at the Highlanders' defenses, he swung wide to avoid that sector, coming at the landing field from another angle. Behind him, on the skyline of the city, a column of black smoke rose straight up in the still air, making an ugly streak against the dawn-fresh sky.

The Steel Wolves held the port, but had not, apparently, expected a lone 'Mech to enter it unsupported. He suspected that they had spotted him early on, and were waiting to see what he would do.

"Any unit, any unit," came a call over the intra-'Mech circuit. The speaker was using one of the Highlander frequencies. "Any unit, request support at grid one-five-three."

Crow reached up and switched off the internal speaker. One-five-three, he thought. The smoke on the skyline would be coming from somewhere near there. One-five-three was in the north-west quadrant, near the suburb of Fairfield, where the Highlanders and the Wolves faced one another across the Tyson and Varney 'Mech factory. He had chosen his route out of the city well.

There were two civilian DropShips grounded at the port. The Wolves had left them alone so far—Anastasia Kerensky was after bigger game. And while she might not approve of a DropShip leaving Northwind at the moment, the odds were that she wouldn't make more than a cursory effort to stop it. With communication these days increasingly dependent upon ships coming and going between planets, nobody wanted to get a reputation for the bad treatment of independent ships and crews.

Whether or not a single MechWarrior making contact with a civilian DropShip would strike the Wolves as a threat serious enough to need stopping . . . that was the question.

The nearest civilian DropShip had the name *Quicksilver* emblazoned on its hull, underneath the image of a winged sandal. The metal surface glittered in the first rays of the early morning sun. The vessel's cargo bay doors stood open, as if the Wolves' descent had caught *Quicksilver* in the act of offloading or taking on cargo, and her captain had opted to defuse hostility by remaining open and defenseless.

Ezekiel Crow walked the *Blade* up to *Quicksilver*'s cargo bay, where a voice hailed him over the ship's loudspeaker.

"*Blade* MechWarrior, this is *Quicksilver*. Identify yourself and state your business."

"I am a Paladin of the Sphere," Crow replied over

the 'Mech's external speakers. "My name is Ezekiel Crow. And in the name of The Republic, I require the use of this ship."

"You are asking me to lift off from a war zone. Will The Republic compensate me for any loss or damage that might result?"

"You have my word," Crow said. By now the irony of such a statement coming out of his mouth scarcely choked him at all.

"And I am a loyal citizen of The Republic. Bring the 'Mech into the bay."

A crewman was waiting inside the dark cargo bay. Using lighted wands, he directed the *Blade* forward toward a cargo cradle. Crow walked his 'Mech the length of the bay to face the cradle, then turned and backed into it. He felt the 'Mech's balance shift as it came to rest against the bulkhead, then relaxed, sighed, and took the *Blade* into hot-shutdown mode. The arms and legs froze in position and the reactor sighed to minimum power drain, with gyros on standby.

He would do a full, proper shutdown later, after they were in space. But for now, time wasn't his friend. The Steel Wolves had undoubtedly spotted him by now, and—if they were feeling particularly bloody-minded, or if they didn't want the word to get out—a Condor tank backed by Elemental infantry could already be on the way, aiming to cripple *Quicksilver* before it could lift. Then there *would* be unpleasant questions to answer.

He disconnected and shed the cooling vest and the neurohelmet, and stood, stretching as much as possible in the cramped cockpit. His back ached. Was it possible he had been that tense? Did betraying another world not come easily?

Rather than answer his own questions—he'd have plenty of time for that level of introspection on the long flight back to Terra—Crow pushed open the access hatch and climbed out of the 'Mech. He'd stripped down to shorts and T-shirt to pilot the 'Mech; as soon as the cold winter-morning air struck his mostly bare skin, he started to shiver.

"Where is the captain?" he asked the crewman who had guided him to his spot, even as a crew of cargo hands began work on adding extra strapdowns and attachment points to the cargo cradle in order to jury-rig proper transport for the 'Mech. Their tools clanged as the bolts went in and the lines tightened. "I need to make arrangements with him for lifting off as soon as possible."

"This way, sir," the crewman responded. He turned and walked toward a hatch. Crow followed.

With the crewman leading, they stepped through an airtight door. Inside the ship the air was warmer, though still chilly to Crow's overheated skin. They went down a long passageway, climbed a ladder, then took a lift up to the maneuvering and control portions of the ship.

"The captain is on the bridge?" Crow asked as they walked.

"No, sir," the crewman responded. "While you were berthing the 'Mech, he asked me to bring you to the first-class passenger lounge. He said he'd be waiting for you there."

I don't have the time for social pleasantries, Crow

thought impatiently. The tea and biscuits can wait until later.

The passageways were nicer here—wood-grained coverings on the bulkheads, carpet over the deck-plates, brass fittings on everything—as befitted a passenger area. The crewman stopped at a door, knocked, and stood aside.

"Through here," he said.

Crow went through the door and into a large compartment containing a polished wooden table, dark green bulkheads with framed pictures hanging from them, and a silver tea service on a sideboard. The DropShip's Captain was indeed seated at the head of the table—and an officer of the Steel Wolves was standing behind him with a slug-pistol in his hand.

Two more Clan Wolf troopers moved from their places beside the door to stand next to and behind Crow, each one taking hold of one of his arms.

"Good morning, Paladin," the officer said. "How good of you to join us. Galaxy Commander Kerensky has asked me to greet you."

"Good morning, Star Captain," Crow replied. "Give the Galaxy Commander my compliments on her economy of effort—I assume she sent teams to all the civilian ships on the field?—and please inform her that I am on business for The Republic of the Sphere, and shall not be impeded."

"You can convey your compliments in person," the Star Captain replied. "My orders are very specific, and do not include leaving without you."

Crow sighed, and relaxed. "I suppose I have no choice," he said, and without pause swung his right leg behind the left leg of the trooper standing to his right. He threw his hip against the man's hip, and felt the trooper's knee snap.

The man yelped, and fell, and Crow used his now-free right hand to grasp the hand of the second trooper, the one who held his left arm.

He spun into position behind the trooper and his left arm snaked up and around the man's throat, bending him back, lifting him from the floor by his windpipe. At the same time Crow pulled the trooper's sidearm from the holster at his belt and raised it, bringing the slug-pistol's barrel up underneath the trooper's right armpit.

The Star Captain raised his own pistol and fired off a snap shot. Crow felt the projectile strike the body of the trooper he stood behind. The man jerked and slumped in Crow's grip. Crow fired back, a double tap. The first projectile took the Star Captain in the chest, the second just under his jaw. He fell.

The entire exchange had taken only a matter of seconds.

Crow let go of the man he held; the trooper's body collapsed to the deck. Still holding the slug-pistol loosely in his right hand, Crow walked forward and around the table where the *Quicksilver*'s Captain sat, and recovered the Star Captain's fallen weapon.

"When a pistol is pointed at his head, a man does what he has to," the *Quicksilver*'s Captain said. "But I'm a loyal citizen of The Republic."

"So he does," Crow agreed, "and so you are. And I think we should depart this planet before the Wolves notice that one of their Star Captains is not reporting back in."

═══ 36 ═══

Tyson and Varney 'Mech Factory
Fairfield suburb
Tara
Northwind
February 3134; local winter

The long, low buildings of the Tyson and Varney 'Mech Factory covered several hectares of the ground in the suburb of Fairfield, to the northwest of the city. At the moment, the 'Mech Factory was anchoring the right side of the Northwind Highlanders' defenses. Sergeant Hugh Brodie lay prone on the frozen ground behind the end of the Mech Assembly Building, with just his head around the corner, binoculars pressed to his eyes.

"Movement," he whispered into his throat mike.

"Squad strength, Gauss rifles, full packs. Steel Wolf urban cammie smocks. No vehicle. Moving toward me in open formation."

"Roger," whispered an answering voice in his headset. "If they pass the halfway point, call in mortars. Else stand fast and report."

"Roger, out."

The sergeant pulled back behind the cover of the wall. "Right, lads," he said to the fire team that clustered there. "Things may get hot in a bit. Check your gear, check your buddy's gear. If anyone's low, now's the time to reload. Prepare smoke canisters. But don't fire until I do."

The fire team members nodded understanding. Sentry and security duty along the interface between Steel Wolves and Highlanders was wearing on the nerves—everybody was tense after a night spent waiting for the heavy fighting to break out, either from a full-scale Steel Wolf assault or from a Highlander counterattack—but these troops were good at what they did. They went through the motions quickly and professionally, with no excess sounds. The sergeant crawled back to his position looking around the corner of the building.

The Wolf troopers were closer, coming up on the midpoint of the long wall. Not a major attack, Brodie thought. Not yet. This looked like just a probe.

"Company, this is Observation Post Five," the sergeant said over his throat mike. "Twelve in the open. Position alpha. Request mortar support."

"Roger."

A thump. A black flower of dirt bloomed along

the road that connected the Steel Wolves' lines with those of the Highlanders.

"Left two, add five, ten rounds, fire for effect," the sergeant whispered. A moment passed. The approaching squad had vanished, taking cover along the walls and in depressions in the ground. They knew what was coming. Veterans of many campaigns, the Steel Wolves, too, were good at what they did.

The ground where the Steel Wolf infantry had stood earlier erupted in more geysers of dirt and smoke. The sergeant pushed himself to his feet, pointed to one of his troopers, then pointed around the corner.

"Let's see what we got," he said.

" 'Kay, sarge," the trooper said, swinging tight around the corner, pressing his body up against the wall.

"Cover him," Brodie said to the rest of the fire team.

The sun was rising, the day would be cold but fair. The trooper dashed forward, his Gauss rifle at his shoulder, the muzzle swinging to follow his eyes.

He froze. "Armor!" he shouted, and dashed back toward the fire team.

"Smoke!" the sergeant shouted. Four canisters rattled as they were thrown, rolling along the road behind the running man.

"Fire!"

The team's weapons shot past their comrade into the screening wall of white smoke. They weren't planning on hitting anything, just on making the enemy keep their heads down and ruining their aim.

The man got back to the corner. "DI Schmitt tank," he reported to Brodie between gasps for breath. "At least one. Plus dismounts."

Damn, Sergeant Brodie thought. Maybe this is the big attack, after all.

"Places, people," he said. "We're going to hold here as long as we can, but fall back. We can't hold against a push on our own." He crawled back to his position observing around the corner. "Company, this is Observation Post Five. Schmitt inbound. Soft targets. Mortar support, free fire, same coordinates."

"Roger."

Once again the crump of mortars sounded from down the street. Mortar rounds wouldn't hurt armor, but would strip away its infantry support and force the tank commander to button up, limiting his vision.

"Walking ladder," the sergeant said. "Add ten. Fire. Drop five. Fire. Add ten. Fire. . . ."

The mortar rounds made a crawling curtain of smoke and fire as they crawled down the street away from the Highlanders' position. The concussions of the mortar rounds, even at this range, felt like punches.

"And here he comes." The Schmitt came through the mask of dirt and flying rubble. It crawled up the street. The tank's main guns swung slowly from side to side. Then the vehicle stopped, rocked over onto its left side, then righted itself. A column of flame shot from the top hatch. A Highlander antitank gun inside the building to the right had fired through an open doorway directly into the Schmitt's side armor at point-blank range.

The wall where the artillery piece hid collapsed as

it was struck by a short-range pulse of energy. Shortly after, a second Schmitt crawled around the burning wreck of its mate.

"More armor inbound," the sergeant said over the radio. "They're taking hits but not turning back. This could be a push."

"Roger," the talker back at Company replied. "Stand fast. We'll try to get some support out your way."

"Wait, wait," Brodie said. "We're going to have to fall back. They're backed by a 'Mech."

"Report!"

"One 'Mech. Industrial mod, MiningMech with machine guns and short-range missiles. Jump-jet infantry accompanies. Steel Wolves combat loadout. Can't tell which unit. Scout car with machine gun for infantry support. Coming this way."

"Roger, Observation Post Five," Company said. "Fall back to the workers' dining hall. Await instructions."

"Roger, out." The sergeant crawled back from the corner, then stood and joined his troops. "Okay," he said, and pointed toward the cafeteria building—perhaps fifty yards away, and still possessing unbroken glass in its many windows. "We're going *there*. Now pop smokes, and let's move."

37

The Fort
Tara
Northwind
February 3134; local winter

The Combat Information Center at the Fort was a windowless, subterranean room packed with map displays, data and communications consoles, and specialists in uniform. Under everyday circumstances it would have been a quiet, even boring place to stand a watch, but with the Steel Wolves at the Drop-Port and a major battle clearly in the offing, the CIC was full of intense but orderly activity.

Captain Tara Bishop had been working in the CIC all night, ever since the Countess of Northwind had sent out Paladin Ezekiel Crow to alert the mercenaries and bring them around into position. That had been a long time ago, as time flowed in wartime, and they still had no word. For some time now, Captain Bishop had been mentally reviewing the varieties of disaster that could have overtaken a single warrior— even a warrior in a 'Mech—while passing through territory supposedly still under friendly control. "Supposedly" being the key word; and Bishop knew that if its implications made her feel concerned about the Paladin's safety, then the Countess of Northwind, under her highly polished diplomatic exterior, must be close to frantic.

The Countess checked her watch. She'd been doing that at roughly five-minute intervals for the past half hour. This time, whatever feelings she was keeping in check behind the Countess-and-Prefect façade finally impelled her to speak. "What's taking Crow so long? Even if it took him longer than it should have to roust Farrell's mercenaries out of bed and get them moving, we ought to have heard something from them by now."

"I don't know what the hangup is, ma'am," Bishop replied. Now was not the time to air her own visions of disaster, when the Countess undoubtedly had her own fears to deal with. "But I'm sure he's got the mercs moving by now."

"I'd be happier if I'd actually heard from Crow that they were moving," the Countess said. "I'd be even happier if anyone had actually *seen* them moving. I'd be happier if . . . a lot of things."

"We'd all be happier if the Steel Wolves took their

anger-management problems elsewhere," Captain Bishop agreed. "But they're here, and we're stuck in hurry-up-and-wait mode."

She picked up the stack of messages from the comm board. Half-a-hundred requested the Countess's action or reply. By now Captain Bishop knew which messages were the ones that the Countess really needed to see, and which were the ones that Bishop could initial and send back all on her own.

None of the messages were from General Griffin, and those were the ones she and the Countess were waiting for, with almost as much eagerness as they waited for Ezekiel Crow to walk back through the door with word that Farrell's mercenaries were moving to flank the Wolves. Catch the Steel Wolves between the hammer and the anvil, with the Highlanders as the anvil, and the sparks they struck would send fire all the way back to Tigress.

"Have you considered sending out a scout/sniper unit to look for Kerensky?" Bishop asked, as she flipped through the messages.

"Considered it, decided against it," the Countess replied. "It comes a bit too close to deliberate assassination, for one thing—not the kind of precedent I'm willing to set—and for another thing it probably wouldn't work. If she isn't at her field headquarters with Elemental infantry three deep guarding the perimeter, then she's out on the line in that *Ryoken II* of hers, and it would take a bigger can opener than a squad of scouts and snipers to cut her out."

A knock sounded at the door of CIC.

"Enter!" Bishop called.

A courier appeared, holding a message. "Ma'am," he said to the Countess. "Compliments of Colonel Ballantrae, northern sector, and the Wolves are jamming our comms."

"That explains quite a lot," Bishop said. "The Countess's compliments to the Colonel and is that all?"

"No, ma'am." The courier offered her a message pouch. "There's some kind of attack going on along the right flank."

"About damned time," the Countess said, as Bishop took the pouch and opened it. "That'll be Farrell's people. Tell the Colonel to stand fast, and allow any Steel Wolves who wish to do so to surrender."

"That isn't it," Captain Bishop said. She'd opened the pouch and begun looking over the hard-copy messages that the courier had brought. "I'm seeing reports of a number of probing attacks in the northeast, but no reports of movement by Farrell's mercs, or anyone else. It's all—"

"Ma'am," the messenger said. "The Colonel requests reinforcements. Or he can't hold. Ma'am."

"Damn," the Countess said. She turned to Captain Bishop. "We can't send reinforcements to the flank without weakening the center of the line. How do you feel about the two of us suiting up and adding some 'Mechs to stiffen the Colonel's spine?"

Captain Bishop smiled, feeling the smile stretch into an eager grin despite her best efforts to remain cool and collected. "To think that when I pulled headquarters duty, I was afraid that I'd never get to see action again."

"You shouldn't have worried," the Countess said. "You're with me." She turned to the courier. "Tell Colonel Ballantrae that help's on the way. If you hurry, you'll get there before we do."

38

Northwest Quadrant
Tara
Northwind
February 3134; local winter

The Highlanders' command post in the northwest quadrant had seen an increasing tempo of operations as night wore on into morning. First radio comms, then messengers brought word of attacks all along the line. The Steel Wolves weren't yet pressing hard, but they were pressing hard enough, and in enough places, that any slackness on the part of the defenders could bring about a break in the line. And a break in the line could become the hole through which the Wolves would pour, rolling up the Highlanders right and left, attacking simultaneously from before and behind and on the flank, leading to a collapse of command and control over all of Tara's northwestern suburbs.

And after the suburbs, the whole city, and after the city, the planet.

" 'Mech approaching," Corporal Shannon MacKenzie reported to her sergeant. "Industrial Mod of some kind."

"One of ours or one of theirs?"

"Theirs, I think," MacKenzie said. "Everything else coming from the east has been theirs. Why not this?"

"Because I'd hate to fry one of our own people. We don't have enough 'Mechs as it is."

Colonel Ballantrae had been listening to the Corporal's report as well, with an expression of increasing grimness. Now he said, "Get me Captain Fairbairn."

Corporal MacKenzie worked the field phone—a primitive model, working off of strung wire, but one not vulnerable to the Wolves' jamming—then passed the handset over to the Colonel.

"Got him, sir."

"Fairbairn," the Colonel said. "There's a 'Mech, up on Lombard Street. One of theirs. Take what you need, do what you have to, but stop it."

"Yes, sir."

Captain Fairbairn put down the field phone. "Well, Sergeant, if you had to stop a 'Mech, how would you do it?"

"Dig a pit, let it fall in. Works in the tri-vids, anyhow."

"I like it," Fairbairn said. "If our city utility maps are right, there's a sewer up under the car park, west of the 'Mech construction hangars. Get demolition rigged under the street, enough to give me a five-meter-deep crater. Command detonated. Nothing showing on the surface. When will you have it?"

"When do you need it, sir?"

"Yesterday."

The sergeant frowned for a moment in thought. "Um . . . twenty minutes, then. Sir."

"Very well. Twenty-one minutes from now there will be a Steel Wolf 'Mech on top of your pile of demo. Blow it."

The sergeant saluted. "Sir."

"Very impressive," Lieutenant Griswold said as the sergeant left. "Now, how are you going to get that 'Mech into place?"

"I have a couple of ideas," Fairbairn told the lieutenant. "We can lure it, or we can drive it. Or some combo of the two."

"Combo."

"Right. Lombard runs north of the car park. We need a tempting target, on the south side of the car park."

"And we need to make sure the 'Mech can't use ranged weapons on it."

"We can do that. There's a disabled Behemoth II at the repair yard. Get it down on the south side of the square, facing south. Put a squad on it making smoke so it's obscured until . . . 0827. At 0827, they will stop making smoke. Got it?"

"I think I see where you're going," Griswold said.

"Then get moving, Lieutenant. You don't have a lot of time to round up a tow to put it in place."

Griswold saluted in turn, and headed out.

"Last thing . . ." Fairbairn picked up the field phone again. "I need a section of flamethrowers on the north side of the 'Mech Factory car park. I want the north side and the west side of the park, and the side streets, covered. If they see a 'Mech, and they will, I want them to flame. Make it happen."

Then he strolled from the storefront he'd been using as a headquarters to the street where a mortar battery was emplaced. Fairbairn walked over to the sergeant in charge.

"Good morning, sir," the sergeant said, saluting.

"Good morning," Fairbairn replied. He looked at his watch. "I have a problem you can help me with. There's a Wolf 'Mech north and east of here. I want to drive it south and west. How much white phosphorus do you have?"

"Thirty rounds," the sergeant replied.

"Get an observer out, and start dropping Willie Pete on that 'Mech. I want him warm."

The sergeant pointed to a man and made a come-hither gesture with his forefinger. The man, a private, approached.

"Hamish," the sergeant said. "Since you're my best observer, and since you don't owe me any money, I have a special assignment for you."

Quickly, he explained the situation to the trooper, who listened with a resigned expression and said, "I want a weekend pass when this is over."

"I'll think about it," the sergeant said. "Right now, you need a place where you can see me and the 'Mech at the same time. The top of the Tyson and Varney water tower ought to do it."

"Just the place if I want to get picked off by a sniper," Hamish said.

"Don't sweat it, Hamish," another trooper said. "The Steel Wolves are all lousy shots."

"I'm more worried about your lousy shooting than about theirs," Hamish said, but he was picking up his kit as he spoke. "Give me a minute, and I'll get you your fix on yon wee beastie."

He loped off, and was soon climbing the access ladder to the top of the Tyson and Varney water tower. The sergeant fixed him with binoculars. Hamish raised his left hand, held up three fingers, then lowered it. He raised it again, with two showing.

"One round, thirty relative, range two hundred," the sergeant said.

"Fire," said Captain Fairbairn.

A trooper holding a round above the mortar let go, and turned away. The bomb slid down the tube, and launched with a thump and a thin cloud of blue smoke. It traveled slowly—a quick-eyed man could follow it in flight.

A crump sounded from the far side of the building.

"Wonderful things, mortars," Captain Fairbairn commented. "Let you shoot over things, so you can't be seen and they can't shoot back."

"Unless they're tracking the trajectory on radar," said the sergeant.

"We'll worry about that later. Nothing we can do about it now."

Hamish, on top of the water tower, pointed up, then raised two fingers. Then he pushed his thumb to the left and raised one finger.

"Add twenty, left one," the sergeant said. Drop. Swish. Thud. Crump.

Hamish made a circle with his thumb and forefinger.

"Willie Pete. Two rounds."

Drop, swish, thud. Drop, swish, thud.

Hamish pumped his fist up and down, then indicated down one, left three. The mortar fire, the burning hot, sticky white phosphorus, went out of the tube, down toward the industrial mod in the far street. The 'Mech was picking up speed, based on Hamish's corrections.

Captain Fairbairn left the mortar section to their work and hastened over toward the car park. There was the Behemoth II, with a haze of smoke shielding it. He could hear the sound of the 'Mech now, the heavy pounding of its feet on the pavement. It was moving fast. It was blinded by the white phosphorus smoke. Between two buildings to the north, it burst out, some burning phosphorus still clinging to its housing. The mortar battery had scored at least one direct hit.

And the 'Mech went running to the west, missiles and machine guns both firing, more heat building up from the burst of speed. Then the flamethrowers concealed in the building beside it lit off, gouts of red flame laced with black rolling over the 'Mech's housing. The 'Mech's machine guns—too damaged, perhaps, to continue shooting—fell silent.

The 'Mech turned, its pilot seeking an open path away from the heat, and the last of the screening smoke drifted away from the decoy tank. The Mining 'Mech's pilot spotted the juicy target—a chance to take out a heavy. The 'Mech pivoted from the hips, the big rock-cutter in its right arm roaring to life, and strode across the open car park in the direction of the decoy tank.

Precisely halfway across the car park, the 'Mech vanished. First it was moving, then the pavement heaved around it, and then after the flying chunks of concrete came to earth there was a crater, but no 'Mech anywhere in sight.

Captain Fairbairn glanced at his watch. Twenty-one minutes precisely.

"Never become predictable," he said aloud, to no one in particular. Then he made his way back to his own headquarters to report.

39

Tara
Northwind
February 3134; local winter

Captain Tara Bishop and the Countess of Northwind
stripped to shorts and T-shirts in the 'Mech hangar
adjacent to the Armory. Even though the walls of the
hangar gave shelter from the wind, the cold February
air raised gooseflesh on Captain Bishop's bare skin.
She bore it stoically, knowing that the cockpit of her
BattleMech would have her sweating soon enough.

Most of her gear she stowed in one of the full-size
lockers in the hangar, as did the Countess, but she
opted to bring her winter uniform greatcoat with her
into the 'Mech's cockpit, even though the bulky garment scarcely fit into the tiny onboard locker. If she

had to dismount from her 'Mech at some point during the upcoming evolution, she would be grateful for an ankle-length coat of heavy wool to go between her overheated body and the winter chill.

Captain Bishop settled into her *Pack Hunter*—a jump-jet equipped hunter-killer, mounted with a particle projector cannon and extended range lasers. The *Pack Hunter* was fast-moving and hard-hitting, a good 'Mech for bringing down enemy units in the open field. The Countess of Northwind preferred her *Hatchetman*, a close-in heavy fighter, armed with an immense, brutal ax. No so fast as a *Pack Hunter*, but deadly once it closed with a foe. The two 'Mechs would complement each other well.

Captain Bishop put on her cooling vest and neurohelmet, and began taking the *Pack Hunter* through the security protocols and start-up sequence. Shortly after she had finished, and had brought the *Pack Hunter*'s fusion engines all the way to life, she heard the Countess's voice over the 'Mech-to-'Mech circuit.

"Up and out on three. One, two, three."

The two 'Mechs turned and walked out of the bay into the morning sunshine. Captain Bishop swung the 'Mech's arms as she strode along, feeling the power in the metal-and-myomer limbs that were so familiar, from long practice, that they seemed like extensions of her own body. She always felt at her brightest and most alive when she was in the cockpit of a 'Mech, and the prospect of action gave her a not-unpleasant adrenaline buzz.

She keyed on the 'Mech-to-'Mech circuit. "Bishop to Campbell, radio check, over."

"Read you loud and clear," the Countess's voice came in return. "How me, over?"

"I read you the same. Want to go out hunting, Countess?"

Captain Bishop wasn't certain, but she thought that she heard the Countess of Northwind laugh. "That's the best suggestion I've heard all day."

Before they had gone more than a few miles, the location of the heaviest fighting became obvious. A pall of smoke hung over the northern end of the town. Bishop and the Countess increased their speed, moving from a steady forward tread to a heavier, fifty-kilometer-per-hour jog. BattleMechs were never inconspicuous, but at the faster pace, their approach would rattle windows and send a tremor through the ground.

"Let them know we're coming," the Countess said over the 'Mech-to-'Mech circuit. "No surprises that way. Sneaking up on a man who's in the middle of a gunfight is a good way to get yourself shot."

Bishop felt the beads of sweat begin to trickle down her forehead as the *Pack Hunter*'s cockpit warmed up. The sensor screens were all bright; the gauges read nominal; the weapons were fully charged and ready.

"I don't know about you," she said, "but I want to kill something."

"I want to see what's going on for myself, first," the Countess said. "I'm not a hundred percent sure that what our man was reporting as an attack isn't really a retreat-in-force."

"We can only hope," Captain Bishop said.

They were closing in on the area of the fighting now. Their own troops were well dispersed, dug in, and ready. Kerensky's Wolves would need luck as well as skill and masses of steel to break through, just as the Highlanders themselves would need luck to hold—luck, because compared to the Highland forces, the Wolves did have masses of steel. Not only that, but their reputation was ferocious.

Captain Bishop wished she could say the same about the Highlander forces currently holding the planet's capital. They had some experienced troops, after last summer's engagements in the Rockspires and on the plains above Tara, but—thanks to that same fighting—they didn't have enough. Not with the Wolves howling for blood. That was why the Countess had worked with Paladin Crow to hire Farrell's mercenaries in the first place, in order to take up the slack until recruitment and training could fill the empty spaces.

Another few moments, and they were through the line and into the thick of the fight. The Countess fired at a Condor tank with Steel Wolf markings, then jumped away from the return volley of short-range battlefield missiles that the Condor's support troops launched back at her.

"Infantry's getting uppity," Captain Bishop observed.

"That's because they can get in close," the Countess said. "We're in a built-up area. They can go above un, got below us, and move out of sight until they're close enough to do real damage."

"Sneaky bastards."

"You won't get any argument on that from me," the Countess replied. "Have you spotted anyone yet besides our own people and the Wolves?"

"Negative. Command and control says: nothing from the mercs."

"Right," the Countess said. Her voice was taut. "Bishop, get over to the mercs' encampment. Find Farrell, ask him where the hell he's been. Get things moving. And if you happen to see a burned-out *Blade* 'Mech along the way—"

"If I do, I'll deal," Bishop said.

She turned her 'Mech and started it loping away. As she ran, behind her, the Countess's *Hatchetman* swung its massive, depleted-uranium ax at a wall, breaking it into a hundred pieces and showering the rubble down onto the invading infantry below.

Then the *Hatchetman* jumped, and Captain Bishop couldn't see it any more.

40

Fort Barrett
Oilfields Coast
Kearney
Northwind
February 3134; dry season

"**W**ill, Jock, Lexa," Master Sergeant Murray said. "Sit down, then."

Will and his two friends had not been back at Fort Barrett more than half an hour before they found themselves summoned to Murray's office—a cubby off the squad bay. Even inside that enclosed and windowless space, they could hear and feel the air around them vibrating at a steady low rumble as aircraft after aircraft took off from the base's landing field, bearing troops to New Lanark and the relief of Tara.

Will glanced over at Jock and Lexa. His conscience was fairly clear—there hadn't been much chance for trouble, going south along the coast and back, and he hoped that theirs were too. His stripes were still too fresh to rip them off now. But an invitation to sit was a good sign.

"What's up?" Jock began, but Murray had his back turned and was pulling a bottle of whiskey from a desk drawer, along with four battered china teacups.

"I know the three of you are friends," Murray said, pouring liberal doses of amber fluid into each of the cups. "Fought together, came up through the ranks together."

"Aye," Jock said, "that's true," and Will and Lexa nodded.

The three of them accepted the filled teacups, and Will sipped at his carefully. It was good liquor—strong and peaty, and meant for thoughtful drinking. If a man wanted merely to get drunk, he spent his money on cheaper stuff.

"And I hear that you're familiar with the Rockspires," Murray said, looking directly at Will.

"There's some that say I am," Will agreed.

"The captain has something special, and I can't think of anyone who'd be better," Murray said. "You can always say no, of course, but if you're the soldiers that I think you are—then you'll be platoon sergeants, and that's an honor for ones so young as you."

Will was getting a bad feeling. A smiling, friendly sergeant, serving drinks and offering an opportunity for advancement . . . he kept silent and waited for the hook at the end of the fishing line.

"Well, then," Murray went on, "knowing the Rockspires as you do, and knowing that the Countess has her castle there, I'm sure you'll be honored as well to be the ones to hold it until she comes to set it up for a new headquarters."

"Things are that bad, back in Tara?" Lexa asked.

Murray nodded. "So I think."

Will hesitated a moment, to hear if Jock or Lexa had anything more to say, but when he looked over in their direction, he saw that they were watching him already, as if waiting for him to speak. He realized that he'd been elected group spokesman without being informed of the vote.

"If that's how it is," he said, "then we're in. For Northwind. And the Countess."

Murray gave a satisfied nod. "You'll have a company, and the captain himself will be with you. Your aircraft leaves in half an hour. And leave your kit behind, all but what you can carry in a fight. You won't need it."

"Good thing I never wasted my paycheck on a pair of those open-toed pumps," said Lexa. "Who knew that I'd be in the army for the rest of my life?"

She slugged back the whiskey and set the empty teacup down on Murray's desk. A second later, Will and Jock did the same. As they left the office, Will noticed that Murray hadn't touched his own drink.

41

Captain Bishop knew the way to One-Eyed Jack Farrell's headquarters, off to the west of the city. The *Pack Hunter* was fast and it was not long before she found herself approaching a roadblock on the city's west side, with a Scimitar MKII locked onto her and tracking.

"I'd like to talk with Captain Farrell," she said over the 'Mech's external speakers.

"He's up the road a ways," the trooper at the roadblock replied. "You want to leave your 'Mech here?"

"I don't think so."

The troops had a whispered conversation. One of them picked up a field phone and called away on it. After a while he got a response.

"Boss says to come on through," he said. "Up the road, Jack'll see you."

Bishop took the *Pack Hunter* up the road until she found Jack Farrell sitting at a table by the roadside, his massive *Jupiter* 'Mech towering empty beside him.

"Come on down," Farrell said. He had a deck of cards in front of him, and was dealing himself a hand of solitaire. Except for his clothing—winter-cammo field gear and a marksman's fingerless gloves—he looked much as he had when she first met him, playing poker aboard the DropShip *Pegasus*.

Bishop hesitated a moment. Then she gave in and retrieved her winter greatcoat from the cockpit locker. Shrugging the coat on over her shoulders, she popped open the 'Mech's hatch and climbed down.

"Take a load off," Jack said, gesturing to the seat in front of him. He scooped up the cards, shuffling them idly without looking at them. "What can I do for you?"

Bishop remained standing. "I'm looking for a bit of information," she said. "Has anyone seen Paladin Crow?"

"Yep." Jack shuffled the cards, cut them, then shuffled again.

"Well, we're waiting," Bishop snapped. "There's an attack going on right now. You're supposed to be doing an envelopment past the right flank."

"Beg to differ," Jack said. "We talked with Crow, all right, and we've got a contract."

Bishop began to feel a sinking sensation in her stomach. "What exactly does the contract say?"

"Well, parts of it are private."

"I believe it's our business as well . . . but never mind. Mostly I'm concerned about the fact that you're ignoring orders from the Paladin. You're supposed to be leading an attack, not sitting under a tree playing with yourself."

Jack chuckled. "But we are fulfilling our contract. Our orders are to sit here, although trees aren't specifically mentioned."

The uneasy sensation in Bishop's stomach turned without warning into a sickening drop, as though the ground she stood on had fallen away, leaving only the gaping pit beneath. This was worse than mercenaries acting . . . well, like mercenaries. This was—"The Paladin ordered that?"

"Yep."

She kept her face unmoved and her voice down in its normal register, even though the effort it took was hard enough to hurt. "I'd like to talk with him."

"Can't do that, either," Jack informed her. "He went through the lines up to the DropPort this morning. DropShip took off half an hour, forty-five minutes later. He's gone. Leaving us to honor our contract."

"I can check on that, you know," Captain Bishop said.

"I know."

"And what, specifically, is your relationship to the Highlanders supposed to be?"

"Specifically," Jack said, "we're supposed to make

sure you don't retreat out of the city to the west. We're to hold you while the Wolves hammer you. Nothing personal, I promise."

"The Paladin is gone," Captain Bishop said. Has deserted us, she wanted to say; has turned traitor and handed us over to our enemies—but there was no point in speaking of treason to mercenaries. "Let's work out a new deal."

Jack shook his head. "He's gone, but the contract's still in force. How would it look if we started ignoring contracts? We'd never get hired by anyone again. Tell you what, though, you're a good kid. You've got a spark to you. And you have a 'Mech. How'd you like to join up with us? Nothing wrong with being on the winning side. Good pay and good chow, too."

"I'm honored," Bishop said, letting the tone of her voice explain that she was actually nothing of the kind. "But I don't think I'll take your offer. How about we cut for it? You get the high card, you stay here. I get the high card, you come with me."

"I don't think much of that," Jack said. "It's one thing in a friendly game. It's another thing when a contract's on the line. But like I said, I like you. Get back in your 'Mech, and you have safe passage back to your own lines."

Captain Bishop bit her lip against a reply. The offer was a generous one by mercenary standards, and if Farrell didn't realize how much of an insult it was by her own, now was not the time to teach him. She stalked back to her *Pack Hunter* in stiff-shouldered silence.

"Don't forget what I said," Farrell stood and called

after her. She paused with her foot on the bottom rung of the 'Mech's access ladder and looked back at him as he continued. "We can always use sharp kids.

"At least, we shouldn't be fighting each other," he added. "I could use a few more like you."

Then he sat again, and redealt his cards.

Captain Bishop ascended the ladder to the *Pack Hunter's* cockpit and spun the hatch closed. As quickly as she could, she put back on the cooling vest and neurohelmet and ran through the primary and secondary security sequences. She had to get back to the city as fast as she could and break the bad news to the Countess.

She pushed her *Pack Hunter* up into the upper range of its speed, keeping it near a hundred kilometers per hour as she took it in great loping strides toward the northeast, where the Highlander line was being pressed. She hadn't used much ammo so far this morning, and her temperature level was fine. She turned to the battle circuit, looking for a place where the timely arrival of a Mech might make a difference.

The amount of radio traffic near the waterworks sounded like things were getting hot down there. She altered her course more to the east, then keyed up a call to the Countess.

"My lady, I have news that's best delivered face-to-face. Where shall we meet?"

No answer came back over the link.

42

Fort Barrett
Kearney
Northwind
February 3134; dry season

General Griffin paced through his temporary headquarters at Fort Barrett, his aide, Lieutenant Owain Jones, by his side.

"I liked fighting on other people's worlds more than I'm enjoying fighting on this one," Griffin said. "And when it's all over, I'm going to declare it a priority to make damned sure we have enough heavy lift capacity to carry our 'Mechs and armor around without DropShips."

"That's a great project for next year," Jones said. "As it is, we've got everything that'll fly all the way to Tara with a soldier on board commandeered. The troops are embarking right now, and Fort Barrett's commander is complaining that we're stripping the continent of defenses."

"If he keeps on complaining," Griffin said, "you can tell him from me that if we don't take everything we can from Kearney, we won't have a world to defend, let alone a continent."

Griffin came to his quarters—a cot walled off with temporary dividers behind a set of file cabinets, since Fort Barrett's visiting officers' quarters was currently as overcrowded as everything else—and pulled his own combat pack out from under the cot.

"Where do you have my 'Mech?" he asked Jones.

"Leaving from south of Benderville by heavy-lift VTOL," Jones said. "It should get to the landing zone before you do. And I took the liberty of dispatching a holding force to Castle Northwind. They're already airborne."

"Good job. But that'll signal the Wolves that we're on the move, so we have to get the rest of this show on the road too. We don't have enough airfields between Tara and the mountains to land everyone, and I don't want to scatter my forces. We'll deal with it as it happens. Give the order to saddle up and ride."

$\equiv$ 43 $\equiv$

Tyson and Varney 'Mech Factory
Northwest Sector
Tara
Northwind
February 3134; local winter

Prefect Tara Campbell and her *Hatchetman* were prowling the grounds of the Tyson and Varney 'Mech Factory industrial park, hunting 'Mechs.

The Steel Wolves had almost as few of them as the Highlanders did, she was sure of it. Ever since Devlin Stone's reforms had taken most of the individually or family owned Mechs out of the picture, full-scale BattleMechs had been uncommon and difficult to obtain. Battlefield seizure was always a workable method—she'd gotten a report of one Wolf 'Mech captured only this morning. The explosives that took it out of action had damaged it too badly for the Highlanders to get any immediate use out of it, but perhaps something could be done with it later.

If, she thought, there was a later.

She jump-jetted over a building—the Tyson and Varney Workers' Assembly Hall—looking around at the top of her trajectory to see with her own eyes what the map display represented. There. The Steel Wolves had a group of three Fox armored cars in position behind the T&V Spring Bearing Plant. Their missiles would be of limited use here inside a built-up area, but if the fighting ever moved to the open ground outside the city, she'd prefer not to face the speedy little vehicles.

She touched down briefly on the street, then made another jump, this time to the top of the Spring Bearing Plant. A downward swipe of the *Hatchetman*'s ax, and an eight-meter hole opened up in the roof. She felt a momentary remorse for the destruction she'd just caused, but didn't let the feeling slow her down. Tyson and Varney could always rebuild their factory later if the Highlanders won this fight; but if the Steel Wolves took over Northwind, the workers at T&V would be building IndustrialMod BattleMechs for Anastasia Kerensky if they were lucky enough to be working at all.

She jumped down through the hole in the roof, into the Spring Bearing Plant.

Dark in here, was her first thought. The plant's interior lights were all off. She switched her viewscreen display over to infrared. Quiet in here, too.

The steady stream of background radio chatter had

ceased, and she realized that the steel in the plant's walls, and in the huge machines used to press spring bearings, distorted magnetic signatures and degraded communications. Well, her commanders would have to work without direct contact for a while.

The trio of Fox hovercraft that she'd spotted earlier had been located to the east, and that was straight ahead of her. She started off in that direction. The *Hatchetman*'s jump-jets would be useless in here, and the overhead was low enough that she had to walk the 'Mech down the length of the room in a half-crouch, and there was no way that she'd be able to take it through the doors at the end. She put on more speed and used the 'Mech's forty-five-ton bulk to go crashing through the wall into the next room.

That was more fun than it probably ought to have been, she thought, just before the infantry group she'd broken in among started hammering. The Gauss rifle rounds went plinking off the 'Mech's Durallex armor. Then one of the Steel Wolf troopers brought up a shoulder-launched missile, firing it in an enclosed space without regard for the danger the rocket blast presented to him and his mates.

The *Hatchetman* shuddered around her when the missile hit. Tara lashed out with the ax in her 'Mech's right hand and the infantry scattered, diving into holes and corridors too small for the *Hatchetman* to follow them.

Well, that was the way of it. She sprinted for the far wall, striking it with her ax just a moment before impact to make a hole she could squeeze through, and crashed into the newly created opening, dropping and rolling, taking light damage but damage none the less, as she broke through into sunlight.

Three Fox armored cars with Steel Wolf markings waited there, as she'd expected, their armored sides wavering in the hot air from their engine exhaust. By the chewed and battered look of the Foxes' armored sides, they'd already seen some hard fighting since moving off the DropPort landing field. Their extended-range medium laser cannons glittered menacingly in the morning sun, and Tara knew that both the lasers and the Voelkers 200 machine guns—two of them per Fox, for a total of six—would be on her in a moment. That much burning light and hot metal flying through the air had a chance of disturbing even a *Hatchetman*, if someone got lucky.

She used her own extended-range laser on the farthest hovercar, and was gratified to see it go up in flames as the beam punched through its armor and struck the vehicle's power plant. The nearest hovercar was spinning for a getaway, its crew reacting to the sudden appearance of a BattleMech in their midst. She slashed at it with her ax, cutting into the edge of the vehicle. It sank to the ground, the raw metal of its side scraping against the pavement and sending up a shower of bright sparks, shining brighter in her still-running IR view screen.

Putting the *Hatchetman* into a squat, she worked the 'Mech's huge left hand under the vehicle's skirt, and heaved it over onto its side. That one was out of the fight, though not beyond salvage. The remaining armored hovercar was withdrawing from the fight and heading away at top speed.

Tara Campbell used her 'Mech's jump-jets to leap

into the air and gain height-of-eye for a firing position. At the top of the leap, she took aim and cut loose with the laser. The Steel Wolf hovercar exploded, even as it turned and fired its lasers and machine guns both in a hopeless final attack.

Beam and bullets together passed harmlessly above her head as she came down from her jump and swatted the overturned second hovercar with the flat of her ax. The blow crushed the body of the vehicle down to a little more than half its former height. Now that one was beyond salvage, too.

Time to leave, she thought. All that bursting through walls had sheared off her 'Mech's external antennae, reducing comm range and adding static to the reports she could hear. She turned the corner, heading back toward the Highlander lines.

And there, waiting in the alley that ran beside the Spring Bearing Plant, was a *Tundra Wolf*—seventy-five tons of jump-jetted, laser-fisted, missile-toting nasty, with the ravening silver-metal wolf's head of the Steel Wolves emblazoned across its torso.

Hatchetman and *Tundra Wolf* jumped simultaneously and met in the air, ax smashing against armor, then tumbled to the ground. Tara Campbell pressed her 'Mech in close, going for a grappling attack. The medium lasers in the *Tundra Wolf's* right arm pressed against the *Hatchetman's* torso on the left side, firing hard, burning into her armor. Tara kicked left to push the attacker away, then spun, sweeping her ax around in a desperate attempt to cripple the other 'Mech's legs.

Then, without warning, the *Tundra Wolf* was surrounded by a cloud of fire and smoke as a *Pack Hunt-*

er's particle projector cannon discharged at close range against its back. The *Tundra Wolf* jumped away, leaping over Tara's head—not attacking, but running, heading at speed back to the Steel Wolves' main force.

"Don't follow!" came Captain Bishop's voice over the 'Mech-to-'Mech circuit. "It's a trick. There isn't going to be a flank attack."

"My comms are fuzzy; say again all after 'It's a trick'?" Tara Campbell's heart was pounding loudly in her ears after the exertion of battle and the narrow escape; that, and the damage done to her 'Mech's communications gear during the recent fighting, made her doubt what she had heard.

"There isn't going to be a flank attack," Captain Bishop repeated. "We've been sold out. By a god-damned Paladin of the goddamned Sphere, if you can believe it. There isn't any mercenary support. Farrell and his troops aren't here to help us—they're here to kill us."

"Understood. No flank attack. Thank you, Captain."

Tara Campbell reached out a hand and switched off the *Hatchetman*'s radio, cutting the 'Mech-to-'Mech connection before Captain Bishop could reply. She would have to turn the communications gear on again soon—people would be waiting for a word from her, and she was still the leader in charge of their defense, even if the unthinkable had happened and they were all betrayed—but for a few minutes, at least, she could grieve for her own, more personal betrayal inside the privacy of the *Hatchetman*'s unre-vealing metal shell.

44

Captain Tara Bishop and the Countess of Northwind approached Colonel Ballantrae's headquarters, and shut down their 'Mechs. They climbed out and walked, sweaty and weary, into the building.

Captain Bishop once again had reason to be glad that she'd brought along her winter greatcoat. The Countess, without one, would have been shivering inside a minute if one of the junior officers hadn't rushed to lend her his. Bishop supposed that having people do things like that for you—or maybe just expecting without thinking about it that people *would* do things like that for you—was one of the perks of being brought up from birth as the future Countess of Northwind.

Not that Captain Bishop would have changed places with Tara Campbell at the moment. There were bad ways and worse ways to have a blossoming romance turn ugly, Bishop supposed, but having your new man abandon not just you, but the entire planet you and he were supposed to be defending— that one set a standard for low behavior that was going to be hard to match. You had to give the Countess credit, though; none of it showed in her face. Any tears she might have shed, had all been shed in the privacy of the *Hatchetman*'s cockpit, and 'Mechs had no eyes to weep.

"Repair what you can," the Countess said to Colonel Ballantrae, first thing on entering. "We'll need to fight again today. Reload. And Captain Bishop has some news."

Bishop knew a cue when she heard one. "The mercenaries are refusing to join our fight against the Steel Wolves," she said. "They say that they're doing it— or rather, *not* doing it—on the orders of Paladin Crow."

The Countess added, thin-lipped, "Which raises the question: Where *is* Crow?"

"I've been asking that same thing ever since you left," Ballantrae said. "I have a sighting from very early this morning, the blocking force in the center. He passed through the lines toward the DropPort, in his *Blade*. He hasn't come back or been seen since."

"So he's gone over to the Steel Wolves," Captain Bishop said. "Who'd have thought it?"

Ballantrae shook his head. "Maybe. Or maybe not. A civilian DropShip lifted from the port around forty-five minutes later."

The Countess of Northwind's lips curled back in a snarl. "Running away. Leaving us to our fate, after first making sure that we couldn't win."

"It's always possible that he left Northwind in order to bring help," Bishop said, in the interest of fairness. "With the HPG net down, we can't just send out a message calling for aid. Somebody has to go look for it in person."

"Stop making excuses for the man," the Countess said. "You yourself told me that he'd ordered Farrell's men to fight against us."

"We don't know for certain that he gave those orders," Bishop said. "Just that Jack Farrell said he did."

"And Ezekiel Crow hired Jack Farrell. The mercenaries were his idea from the beginning."

"The devil take him, then," said Colonel Ballantrae. "Him *and* The Republic of the Sphere. If this is how they treat their friends, we're better off without both of them."

"Northwind against all?" The Countess's voice was bitter. "What makes us better than the Steel Wolves then?"

"Damn," said the Colonel, with feeling.

"We're going to catch up with Ezekiel Crow," the Countess promised. "When we do, he and I will discuss the matter. And after our discussion, there'll be need for only one cup and saucer at teatime." She drew a deep breath, and Captain Bishop could sense her resolve to consider the subject closed. "On to other matters, then. What about General Griffin?"

"He's signaled that he's rolling," Colonel Ballantrae said. "With everything that he's got, or at least, everything that he can send."

"How much?"

"Without the gear that's too heavy for air transport—not enough for a pitched battle against the mercs and the Wolves, out in the open."

"Not enough to save the city, then," the Countess said. "But enough to break us out, maybe, and let us hole up in the Rockspires until the Highlanders offworld can launch a counterattack."

"Any reports yet of attacks from Farrell's mercs?" Bishop asked Colonel Ballantrae.

The Colonel shook his head. "That's a negative."

"When will Griffin be here?" the Countess asked.

"Twelve hours."

"I once asked him for a day," she said. "Now it's time for me to give him that day back."

"What do you mean?" Bishop asked.

"I'm going to talk to Anastasia Kerensky, woman to woman," the Countess said. "Send her the message. Ask for a parley."

45

Steel Wolf Field HQ
Tara DropPort
Tara
Northwind
February 3134; local winter

So far, Ian Murchison had spent the battle for Tara in the sick bay on Anastasia Kerensky's DropShip, talking shop with the Steel Wolf medics to keep his mind off what was going down outside, and helping with the casualties as they came in. That much, at least, he could do without a conflict of loyalties—injured flesh was injured flesh, no matter which side it belonged to. So far, casualties had been light. The Steel Wolf medics didn't say, but Murchison understood enough to know that this meant only that the big push into the city was yet to come.

He was assisting a Steel Wolf medic named Barden in the messy job of inserting a tube into a sucking chest wound when Anastasia Kerensky strode into the sickbay. He didn't register her appearance until they had finished punching through the patient's chest wall and inserting the tube. Then he looked up and saw her standing in the doorway, her arms crossed, glaring at them impatiently.

Barden sketched a salute—not even a Steel Wolf Clansman was foolish enough to give the full thing when his latex-gloved hand was still slick with blood and other bodily substances. Murchison, for his part, gave the curt but respectful nod he'd come around to using in lieu of anything more formal and military.

As usual, it seemed to satisfy her. "Bondsman Murchison."

"Yes, ma'am?"

"Make yourself presentable. The Countess of Northwind summons me to parley, and I want you standing with me when she comes."

"Stage-dressing, ma'am?"

Across the examining table from him, Barden looked shocked. Murchison, however, had come to understand that the only way to keep Anastasia Kerensky's respect—and her respect, so far as he could tell, was all that had kept him alive in the first place—was to push back as hard and as often as custom and the broad gap between their ranks allowed.

"An object lesson, Bondsman. Get moving—we have not got much time."

Anastasia's impatience was enough for Barden to let Murchison clean up and change in the sick bay locker room, and to bring him clean clothes to replace the bloodstained scrubs that he'd been wearing when she arrived. His hair was still damp from the shower when he joined her outside the sickbay door, but she only flicked her gaze up and down him once and said, "You will do. Come."

The parley turned out not to be live and face-to-face at all, but done over real-time tri-vid link—neither commander, it seemed, was willing to leave her own territory, and the streets of the city did not offer much in the way of open neutral ground. Despite Anastasia's impatience, the setup took time. The Steel Wolf technicians set up their tri-vid cameras and sound equipment in her field headquarters out on the DropPort landing field, with a full-size display unit that looked too big to have come with the DropShips at all—Murchison suspected that the techs had appropriated it from one of the passenger waiting lounges in the captured DropPort concourse.

Finally, the prep work was finished. Anastasia Kerensky took her position standing on an X that the Steel Wolf technicians had marked on the landing field tarmac, with Murchison standing a little behind her and to the right.

The Steel Wolf technician in charge said something in a low tone over her headset voice pickup—presumably to her Highlander opposite number—and then, more loudly, "On the air in three, Three . . . two . . . one . . . time."

The display unit clouded, swirled, and cleared to show the Countess of Northwind and another officer—

some kind of aide, Murchison supposed—standing in an impressive stone-and-wood great hall that matched pictures Murchison had seen of the Fort at Tara. The Steel Wolf tech fiddled with her controls and brought the image up closer, until Anastasia and the Countess might have been standing only feet apart.

Anastasia Kerensky said, "Countess."

"Galaxy Commander." Tara Campbell's voice and expression gave away nothing; Murchison couldn't tell from her demeanor whether the day was going well or ill for the Highlanders in the city.

"You called for this parley. Say what you have to say—we waste time, otherwise."

At this, Tara Campbell gave a grim smile. "I wasn't born yesterday, Galaxy Commander. Your troops will appreciate the breathing space as much as mine. And we can always go back to killing each other when we're done." She seemed at this point to notice Ian Murchison for the first time, and spoke to him directly. "You're no Steel Wolf, man—not with that Northwind face on you. What's your name?"

"Ian Murchison, ma'am. Medic for Balfour-Douglas Petrochemicals."

"Interesting," said Tara Campbell. "And how did the Galaxy Commander come to add a Balfour-Douglas medic to her collection?"

"The same way that I plan to add Northwind," Anastasia Kerensky said. "Ian Murchison is my Bondsman, taken in battle."

"Going back to the old ways, are you?" Once again, the Countess's gaze shifted to meet Murchison's. "I'm sorry I can't do anything for you directly,

Ian Murchison. Deal honorably with the Galaxy Commander—and if she fails to deal honorably with you in return, I'll add that to the score I have with her when the time comes to settle all our debts."

"Yes, ma'am," Murchison said—but Anastasia was already speaking, overriding his voice with a hot edge of temper in her own.

"I will deal honorably with my Bondsman because he *is* my Bondsman, Countess, not because of any fear I have of you! And I tell you again, stop wasting my time. Do you wish to surrender?"

"Hardly, Galaxy Commander. Do you?"

"You know full well that I do not. What is your purpose, then?"

Tara Campbell said, "I'm offering you a deal. You and yours can depart from here without pursuit, and we'll call this round a draw—there'll be no retaliatory attacks on Clan Wolf enclaves or Clan-influenced worlds, and no sanctions in the Senate, and the Steel Wolves can go on wreaking havoc anywhere they like so long as it isn't Northwind."

"Do you think that I am a fool?" Anastasia was still angry; Ian Murchison could see the hot color in her cheeks. He wondered if Tara Campbell had deliberately insulted her, or if the slap at her honor had been made in the heat of the moment, after the Countess had seen a fellow-Highlander wearing a Bondsman's cord. "If I win here, I have all that, and without leaving an enemy at my back. No—but because I am a generous and civilized person, I have a counteroffer. Stand down, disarm your forces, and surrender Northwind to me, and you can keep your rank as Countess and your castle in the mountains, so long as you go to it and stay there and never bother me again.''

"No."

"You are outnumbered and unprepared to resist. One more time: will you surrender?"

"You already have my answer."

"Then I tell you, Countess," said Anastasia Kerensky, "I will conquer your planet, and I will kill you, and I will take your pretty stone castle and I will make it into the stronghold of Clan Wolf on Northwind, and the day will come when no one will remember that a woman named Tara Campbell ever set foot in that place. Do you understand me now?"

The Countess of Northwind was pale as white marble, even in the tri-vid display, and her eyes were like cold blue fire. "You can try, Galaxy Commander—you can try." She made a quick slicing gesture with one hand, directed at someone off-display. "Tara Campbell, out."

46

Landing Zone; Jack Farrell's Mercenary
Encampment
Plains North of Tara; Plains Outside Tara
Northwind
February 3134; local winter

"**O**ffload! Offload! Move it, people!"

"Soon's everyone's out, push the bird off the edge of the runway. We have another coming in, three minutes, guys. Move!"

The sky was clear, and the landing field between the Rockspires and the capital city of Tara was crowded. Soldiers, all of General Griffin's troops, were forming up in ranks, units regrouping, ready to march.

The airport itself looked trampled and tramin all parts and all ways. The troops had even stripped the newsstands of hot dogs, bottled water, and popular magazines. In front was chaos, only organized if one was able to recognize a certain by-the-numbers chaos that a well-trained military can sustain for as long as necessary to get the job done.

Squads were out requisitioning everything that could roll on wheels and carry troopers or equipment for a push toward the city. Others were securing checkpoints and communications gear. Above everything, the voices of sergeants with lungs of brass and vocal cords of leather pounded out orders—go here, do that, get ready, stand by, check your gear, move out! Move, move, move! You aren't getting paid by the hour!

General Griffin with his 'Mech—one of three they had, the other two being unarmed ConstructionMechs that the newly arrived forces had requisitioned on the spot—was helping to pull newly arrived aircraft off the field and out of the way, so that the ones still incoming could land. Nothing else besides the 'Mechs had the speed or the power to do the job, and Griffin as the commanding general had nothing else to do, and no decisions to make at this point.

His battle plan, like all battle plans, resembled nothing so much as a spring-wound toy. Griffin had set it into motion, and now he could only watch as the [plan] lurched forward on its own. Maybe later— [no] plan lasts beyond first contact with the [enemy—h]e would need to choose again between pos- [sibilitie]s of action. But until that time came, he [worked] with his hands like a stevedore.

"General," came the voice over the 'Mech's cockpit speakers. "First battalion is formed. Request permission—"

"Permission granted," Griffin said, without pausing in his efforts to pull a transport out of the way, off the tarmac, while another, still-laden transport was coming in behind him. "Carry out your orders."

"Sir."

The afternoon progressed. Local weather reports were calling the weather fair and mild for February, although Griffin knew that many of his Kearney-acclimated troopers would be feeling the effects of the cold. He, at least, wouldn't have to worry as long as he was working inside his 'Mech. At last the final aircraft was down.

"What now?" his aide asked him.

"Set demolition charges," Griffin replied. "No retreat. No spoils for the Wolves if they win. We're going east at speed. Inform me of first contact. Nothing else matters."

He was already taking the *Koshi* eastward at a fast lope, near enough to red-line to be worrisome if he were the kind to worry. He'd have a chance to let the 'Mech cool down once he reached the head of the column. Until then, his place was up front, and the sooner he got there, the better.

"Nothing past here but scouts and skirmishers," the colonel in charge said, when Griffin reached the moving collection of odds and ends at the pointy end of the stick.

The first troops in line had been packed into buses commandeered from the airport for the purpose, and were traveling behind a dump truck with a long-range heavy laser strapped into place on the truck bed with chains and heavy ropes. The colonel himself rode in the front passenger seat of a limousine hovercar requisitioned off the lot at the airport rental company. The hoverlimo's capacious rear seating area had been given over to a complete field communications setup, technician included.

"We'll be at Tara around dusk," Griffin said. "We're moving fast. Punch a hole through to the Countess, consolidate forces. Then we'll see what she wants to do."

"You have an opinion on that?" the colonel asked.

"Fight them."

"You're not going to get much argument there."

"Report coming in," said the communications specialist. "Scouts have reached the edges of Tara. Reporting city held against them."

"Wolves?" Griffin asked. "On this side?"

"The scouts don't think so. But whoever it is, they've got a *Jupiter*."

"Just what I needed to make my day complete," Griffin said. "Carry on."

The relief column continued to the east.

"You want us to do what?"

"You heard me," Jack Farrell said to his second-in-command.

When the mercenary force's farthest-out pickets had brought in reports of a large force approaching Tara from the west, Farrell had reacted by summoning his officers to a council of war. They had gathered at the ad hoc command post he'd set up earlier by the foot of his *Jupiter* 'Mech, and he had presented them with his decision. The logic of it was taking a while to sink in.

Patiently, he went over it all again. "You will defend against the Highlanders coming in from the west to the minimum. You will shoot to miss. On receiving any kind of fire at all, you will pull back and open a corridor."

"What about our contract?" his segundo asked.

"Under our contract," Farrell said, "we've been ordered to secure the roads out of Tara against the Highlander forces in the city, and not to fight against the Steel Wolves unless or until the Steel Wolves first attack us. There's nothing either in our orders or in our contract that says what we should do about any other forces that might decide to join in on the action—which leaves that decision up to me. And I say that our contract never covered being caught between the upper and the nether millstones with the Highlanders turning the mill."

"It's not going to look good, though."

"That's crap and you know it," Farrell said. "Trooper for trooper and 'Mech for 'Mech, our happy bunch of heavily armed misfits are as tough and as brave and as nasty as any Northwind Highlander or Steel Wolf Clansman in The Republic of The Sphere. But anybody wanting us to hold out to the last man has to say so up front and make the contract worth it for our next of kin, and our current employer didn't. No shame to him, either; there aren't many employers out there who'll go that far."

"Bannson would," said his segundo.

"Which is why we'd do it for Bannson if he paid us to," Farrell agreed. "But that's for another contract and another war. Right now, we're working on fulfilling this one without getting chewed to bits in the process."

He looked around at his commanders. "Are we all singing off of the same sheet of music now? Good. Then here's the deal: We'll give the Highlanders an impressive show. I want to hear explosions and I want to see fireworks. But I do not want casualties—no casualties among our troops, and minimal among the others. Let them know they've been in a fight, but no more than that. Am I making myself clear?"

"We don't let the Highlanders inside the city out," his segundo summarized. "But if the Highlanders outside the city happen to force a corridor . . . well, that has nothing to do with us, and what they decide to do with it is their business."

"That's the general idea," Farrell said. "Now we're going to go out and apply it. Carry on."

The meeting dispersed, and Jack Farrell turned away to where his *Jupiter* was waiting. He climbed up the access ladder to the cockpit. His primary employer had left him a great deal of discretion in dealing with his current contract holder, and he hoped that he was exercising it sufficiently now.

Once in the cockpit, he donned the cooling vest and neurohelmet and brought the hundred-ton *Jupiter* rumbling to life. Then he turned its ponderous footsteps onto the road heading west, to see for himself what was approaching.

47

"**C**ontact," said the observer for the mercenary rocket battery.

The mercs currently blocking the roads out of Tara had received some strange orders in their time, and the ones they fought under now were stranger than most. But they'd learned to trust Jack Farrell's one eye when it came to looking out for the main chance, and they obeyed. Not without questioning—that wasn't in their nature—but they obeyed.

"Where away?" said the sergeant in charge of the battery.

"Looks like a light armored truck, mounted laser, hull down past that rise."

"Got it," the sergeant said.

A moment later the observer asked, "Inform Jack yet?"

"Yeah, just passed it back."

"Okay . . . I see one, two, three squads, jump armor, with flamers. They're doing squad rushes."

"We'll let 'em know we spotted 'em," the sergeant said. To the crew of the rocket battery, he said, "Short-range missile. Two pairs, aim two short, two long."

"Missiles away," said the leader of the battery crew.

With trails of white smoke, the missiles arched up and out. The laser tracked them. One exploded in midair, then a second, a third just above the ground, the fourth—one set to go long—impacted out of sight.

"Tubes expended," said the battery crew leader.

"Fall back," the sergeant said. "That'll slow 'em some."

"General," Lieutenant Owain Jones reported over the command circuit. He'd had to leave behind the Joust tank in which he usually shadowed Griffin's *Koshi*, and was riding in a Fox armored car. "We're meeting resistance."

"How much, and where?" Griffin asked.

"So far, it's light. No KIAs on our side. Our troopers are returning fire."

"Do not slow down," Griffin ordered. True to his own words, he kept his 'Mech striding onward in the direction of the city as he spoke. "Not for any reason. The line we're facing will not be thinner at any time. If we don't punch through now, we won't punch through at all."

"I'll pass the word along."

"Good. Has anyone got comms with the Countess?"

"We had a brief contact earlier," Jones said. "There was a parley, but it didn't go anywhere. The forces in the city are bracing for a Steel Wolf push."

"What about the units we're encountering here?"

"Mercs," said Jones. "They've got the Countess and her people pinned, but nobody seems to know if they're going to coordinate an attack with the Wolves or not."

"If we have anything to say about it," Griffin said, "then the answer is 'not'."

Ahead smoke was rising. Griffin headed that way. The *Koshi* swiveled its head from side to side as he advanced at a lope to provide some heavier support than the infantry could manage on their own. He found a squad hunched behind a wall, with small arms fire coming in overhead—deadly stuff for the unarmored infantry, but nothing that would trouble him.

He stepped around the corner and laid down a spread of missiles in the direction the fire was coming from. The front of a building exploded into rubble.

"Move out!" Griffin commanded, then sprinted forward himself. "Move it up, people. Open a hole, and form a perimeter, north and south."

"We have a Condor, grid nine-one-four."

"I'm on it," Griffin said. "Now I want some speed here. Punch through!"

One-Eyed Jack Farrell sat atop his *Jupiter*—not inside the cockpit, but under the open sky, perched on the 'Mech's shoulder and using its great height as a vantage point for observation. He wore a set of communications headphones, with a wire trailing back into the 'Mech's interior.

"Roger that," he said over the headphones' audio pickup. "One *Koshi*. Any other Mechs?"

He paused to listen. "Right, let it past. If I want it, it'll be mine."

From far off to the north of where he was perched, looking out over the nearby buildings from atop his thirty-meter mount, Jack could hear the crump of explosions. Trails of smoke and the exhaust of missiles drew white lines against the blue winter sky.

"Very well," he said over the audio pickup. "Yes, open a corridor. I'll be along shortly."

He took off the headset, rolled up the cable, and slipped into the *Jupiter* through the entry hatch. Once inside, in the seat with vest and helmet, with the 'Mech's electronics fired up, he called back to his ground comms station.

"There's a Highland officer doing perimeter patrol over to our east," he said. "Riding a *Pack Hunter*. Get in touch with her."

"That'll be tough."

"That's okay," Farrell said. "I trust you."

He fired up the reactor and set off, with the *Jupiter*'s slow, deliberate pace, to the north.

*   *   *

Captain Tara Bishop looked down from the cockpit of her *Pack Hunter* at the man in front of her. He was dressed in a mercenary's uniform, with a white flag—she thought, upon closer inspection, that it might be somebody's T-shirt—hanging from a stick he was holding above his head. Two Highland troopers had him at rifle point. They were both standing well back from him, staying out of each other's lines of fire, as well as keeping out of hers.

"You say you have a message?" she said. "Let's hear it."

"One thirty-six dot two," the man said. Her 'Mech's external mike picked it up.

"What's that mean?" she demanded.

She had no patience at the moment for cryptic statements—she was tired and cranky, and the day that had started out badly had not gotten any better as it wore on. The parley with Anastasia Kerensky had been an almost unmitigated disaster—"almost," because it did succeed in wasting the Steel Wolves' time, but disastrous all the same. The Countess of Northwind had broken the link in a state of incandescent fury, white to the lips and cursing Anastasia Kerensky in terms that Bishop hadn't suspected that she knew.

The man shrugged. "I don't know. I was asked to carry that message to you. That's all."

"Take him to the rear," Bishop ordered. As the Northwind troopers marched him off, she pondered for a moment then dialled a frequency into her 'Mech-to-'Mech circuit: 136.2.

"Radio check," she said.

"Hello," came back a male voice. She's heard that

speaker before, at the mercenary encampment, and on the DropShip *Pegasus* before that: Jack Farrell.

"What do you want?" she asked.

"How do you feel about cutting the cards?"

"What's that supposed to mean?"

"You against me," Farrell said. "Your 'Mech to mine."

"A *Jupiter* against a *Pack Hunter*?" Captain Bishop struggled between fear and skepticism. A match like that was straight out of the tales of the old days, when 'Mechs ruled the battlefield and Warriors took and answered challenges that settled the fate of worlds. It was also one-sided to the point of suicide; a *Jupiter* outmassed a *Pack Hunter* by seventy tons, and it carried more and heavier long-range weapons. There was no safety for the smaller, lighter 'Mech either in grappling or in standing off and shooting; the *Pack Hunter*'s only advantages lay in heat efficiency and speed. "Why the hell should I?"

"Because if you win, I'll let you live."

"I'm living fine right now."

"Ah, ah, ah," Farrell said. "You, and the Countess, and all your troopers. There's a relief column coming from the west. I can let them through, or cut them off. I can let you out with them—fight another day, you know? Or I can bottle the lot of you up together for Wolf meat."

Oh, but that was tempting. Even if it meant her death—but she was probably going to die in the city anyway, if the Highlanders stayed pinned between the mercs and the Steel Wolves. This was a chance to buy safety for everyone, and to buy it not with gritty, squalid street fighting against infantry and thin-skinned light armor, but with a death duel against the biggest and most deadly of 'Mechs. Too good, almost, to be true. . . .

"Why should I believe you?" she asked.

"We've played cards. My word is my bond."

"So we have"—and we both cheated, she thought, and we both know it—"and so is mine. Let me talk with the Countess."

"Don't take too long. I have a *Koshi* in my sights right now."

"Five minutes. Ten at the most."

"I can shuffle the cards that long," Farrell said. "Then it'll be time to cut the deck."

48

Road out of Tara
Northwind
February 3134; local winter

The Countess of Northwind, Captain Bishop soon discovered, was less than enthusiastic about Jack Farrell's proposal.

"Right," the Countess's voice said, over the encrypted command circuit in the cockpit of Bishop's 'Mech. "I'm expected to trade your life for . . . what, exactly?"

"All of Northwind," Bishop said. Now that she'd made up her own mind, she'd moved from fearful anticipation into a state of calm, if adrenaline-charged, resolve. "And my life isn't any more valuable to me than the life of the youngest private in the army is to him. Or her. I haven't checked. At any rate, it's what we all agreed to when we signed up."

"If that's what we all agreed to when we signed up, then I should be the one out there taking on a *Jupiter* in a light 'Mech, and not you. And you can get back in touch with Farrell and tell him so. If he wants a duel, he can fight my *Hatchetman*."

"Sorry, ma'am, but no." Bishop kept her voice firm. "Only one death wish at a time allowed in this conversation, and I've got mine already."

"Damn it, Captain . . . do you have any idea how hard it is to break in a new aide-de-camp? And you're one of the best I've ever had."

"Thank you, ma'am. My old colonel said I'd see plenty of action if I served with you. When this war is finished, you can tell him for me that he was right."

"I can't talk you out of this?"

"Afraid not, ma'am."

Over the circuit, Bishop heard a sigh. "Then make the signal," the Countess of Northwind said. "You have my permission."

"Thanks," said Bishop, and retuned her 'Mech-to-'Mech circuit to the frequency she'd used to contact Jack Farrell. "You have a deal," she said over the radio.

"My deck," said Farrell. "My shuffle. My cut."

"I said you had a deal."

"Then meet me within sight of the DropPort. Me in my *Jupiter*, you in your *Pack Hunter*, if you dare."

"I'll be there," she said, and cut the connection.

All that was left now was the chatter on the 'Mech-to-'Mech circuit, as the Countess and the Highlander

forces within the city prepared to move out and take
to the roads heading west.

". . . Head 'em up and move 'em out" . . . "Leave
a line. The sick and wounded" . . . "Automatic and
robotic weapons next to the DropPort; don't let Kerensky know that we've gone. . . ."

The first thing that Captain Bishop noticed was the
magnetic anomaly detector indicating a bearing of
045 relative with signal increasing. Something metal,
something big, approaching from her right front. The
next thing that she noticed was the rhythmic shock-
waves, also increasing in strength, of a hundred-ton
mass approaching at a strolling pace—if a thirty-
kilometer-per-hour rate was a stroll. Her instruments
detected the shock waves first, but soon it was as if
she could feel them through the hull of her *Pack
Hunter*.

Her back was to the DropPort and the Steel
Wolves. Ahead of her lay Jack Farrell's mercenaries.
And sandwiched between them—the Highlanders.
As long as Captain Bishop kept on fighting, the Highlanders could keep escaping. The Countess of Northwind had a thin line of sick and injured volunteers,
armed with robotic and automatic weapons, creating
the illusion of a solid front. Farrell had promised an
escape path for the others.

If he wasn't lying. If he wasn't carrying out a massive ruse of war, luring all of them to a place where
he could disarm or kill the Northwind army.

Nothing for it. She'd made up her mind to meet
him here, to fight him here, and . . . she saw the
approaching 'Mech, a looming, ponderous giant. Jack

Farrell's *Jupiter*. Huge. Heavily armored. She doubted that even her particle projector cannon could hurt it.

Well, maybe not from the front. She was fast. He was slow. If that was going to be her only advantage, she'd have to make the most of it.

She'd been daydreaming too long. The alerts in the 'Mech's cockpit yelped at her, warning that she'd been locked on by hostile fire control. A moment later, a volley of long-range missiles leapt out toward her. Red lights flashed in the cockpit.

"I know, I know," she said aloud, and put the *Pack Hunter* into a run toward the *Jupiter*. She cut to the right, faked left, then halted, braced, and aimed with her micro lasers. Accuracy, she thought, don't fail me now. At the same time she keyed up the mike and broadcast on frequency 136.2, "Heya, big guy. Happy to see me?"

"Delighted," came the response. "You know I'm a sucker for a pretty face."

"Of course you are." The missiles he'd fired exploded harmlessly, but close enough that the fragments spattered against her 'Mech's exterior armor. She sprinted forward again, this time at a diagonal. The *Jupiter* turned to follow. Another battery of missiles sprang from the big 'Mech's torso-mounted boxes, left and right.

Good, Bishop thought. Keep going like that and you'll use up your long-range stuff while I'm still out here

She backtracked. No sense being predictable. Even once the missiles were expended, he'd still be carrying two particle projector cannons to her one.

Missiles incoming. Lasers up. Shoot. Two of the

missiles in the battery vaporized as the laser beams hit them. The others went wide, sending shock waves through the air around her but missing the *Pack Hunter* itself. Either I'm better than I ought to be at dodging those things, Bishop thought, or Jack Farrell is a really lousy shot.

The running and the laser expenditure, however, had sent her heat gauge up a bit. Nothing close yet to redline, but enough to register.

"So that's your game," she muttered. "Get me all hot and bothered."

"And easy pickings," came the answer over the radio, and she realized that she'd left the private 'Mech-to-'Mech frequency open. "Care to dance?"

Another battery of missiles inbound. She dodged and ran, using her 'Mech's agility and speed to take her out of the way of the missiles' ballistic trajectory.

"Don't go too far!" came Jack's voice. Even over the scratchy connection, she could tell that he was laughing at her.

"Not much chance of that," she said. "I'm having a good time right here."

She set her lasers on continuous fire, and concentrated on her shooting. Then she spotted another battery of missiles inbound and jumped, straight up, at maximum burn. The missiles exploded below her. She landed hard, going down onto one knee.

The *Jupiter* was continuing its forward stroll. Now its extended-range particle projector cannon started firing—and about damned time, Bishop thought; if I were riding a *Jupiter* I'd have been chewing up the landscape with my PPC from the moment the enemy came in sight.

The cannon's hot particles burned a fiery path through the air from Farrell's 'Mech toward hers. Well, she'd see about that. She ran toward him, bobbing left and right. The particle beam crossed her legs with a thud she could feel. Then she was jumping, taking herself up and over, and coming down feet first with a shouted war cry, making herself into a thirty-ton battering ram heading straight down onto the *Jupiter*'s head.

"Hey!" Farrell said. "That isn't in the tactics manual for a *Pack Hunter*."

"Neither is surrender," she said. "At least not in mine."

She was behind him now, and she set her eight microlasers to firing at a single spot. The spot that she chose was the back of the fighting machine's left knee. She remembered her old unarmed-combat instructor explaining to the new students, "You can always reach a knee."

Her own PPC added to the scrum. The *Jupiter* started to turn. She turned with it, staying behind, working to keep herself out of reach of the weapons mounted on the larger 'Mech's arms and torso. She could keep this up forever, she thought, jumping and firing and dodging out of reach to fire and jump again, shooting at Farrell until she burned through his armor, or until the heat overloaded him so much that his 'Mech had to shut down to cool off.

She let a brief fantasy cross her mind: the *Jupiter* frozen, herself dismounting her own 'Mech to walk across and take possession. Hauling Jaul Farrell out into the open, maybe killing him, maybe letting him go. Then getting aboard the *Jupiter*, picking up her

Pack Hunter, and walking back to the Countess of Northwind with a fine gift.

Without warning, the *Jupiter* fell over backwards onto the ground. What? she thought. Gyro error? Overheated in the midst of walking and stumbled over his own feet?

Time to get fancy. She darted forward, swinging the ponderous bulk of her *Pack Hunter* into a thirty-ton handstand, and from there into a somersault. She ended by sitting athwart the chest of the fallen *Jupiter*, its arms pinned to its sides by the knees of her 'Mech.

With her knees pinning the *Jupiter*'s arms so that its deadly autocannon couldn't come into play, provided she could keep him down long enough given that he had a seventy-ton weight advantage . . . she switched to the Highlanders' general frequency and called, "Get me a squad with boarding tools out here pronto!"

Then she switched back to the private 'Mech-to-'Mech frequency, even as she leaned forward so that the lasers on her chest pointed directly into the viewscreens of Farrell's cockpit.

"Surrender, Farrell?" she whispered. She flipped the lasers on, a brief pulse, a warning. His faceplate glowed crimson with the effect. Her 'Mech's powerful gripping hands were pressing down on his shoulders. "Or I'll make you do dreadful things."

He kicked up with his legs, both at once, trying to buck her off. She rode him, sliding down to press the *Jupiter*'s hips to the pavement while still keeping his shoulders under the *Pack Hunter*'s hands.

"Naughty," she said. She flipped on the lasers

again—a bit longer burn this time—and gave him a brief burst from her PPC. "I can get angry."

"I'm not worried," Jack said. He didn't sound worried, either.

"Then let's cut for it."

"Let's."

He rolled to the left. She was under him now, and he was pressing her down. She felt the hot blast of his extended range PPC firing, the particles boiling chips off of the concrete beside her face.

He's playing with me, damn it, she thought. You'd think he *wanted* that one to miss!

"Enough," she said. She reached up with her arms and pulled him in close, firing her cannon and all her lasers with their apertures pressed against his armor. She fired them continuously until she felt the *Jupiter*'s body stiffen in her grip, the big 'Mech's inferior heat dissipation unable to keep up with the energy release.

The *Jupiter* relaxed its grip and fell off her to her left with the sort of ground-shaking concussion that only a hundred-ton heavy could make, and lay on its back unmoving. Bishop rolled to her right, got one of the *Pack Hunter*'s knees under its torso, and pushed herself up to a standing position.

"Do you surrender?" she asked.

"Not yet," he replied. "My troops are heading here right now."

"How many more of the Highlanders are there left to get through the lines?"

"Just yourself," he said, "and those gutlwul lads with the can openers, if they get here in time. The rest of your people ran away as if they were experts.

And you're in no condition right now to take on the whole of my mercenary force."

"I took *you* on," she pointed out.

"True," he said. "But you had functioning weapons then. Now you have melted steel all over the fronts of your lasers. They won't fire. And your cannon doesn't look very good either. So what'll it be? Do you want to be captured, or run?"

"I still beat you," Bishop said.

"Yes, yes," Farrell agreed. "We cut the cards and you turned up the jack of spades, just like you did before."

"Just like I did bef— Damn it, Jack Farrell, you *threw* this fight!"

"Bright girl. You figured it out. Now I'm about to give the order to close the corridor. So get moving."

Bishop ran. The infantry squad with its boarding tools saw her coming toward them, and turned and ran as well. At over a hundred kilometers an hour, she didn't take long to reach her lines, on the other side of the city from the DropPort.

The whole way there, Jack Farrell laughed in her headset.

49

Castle Northwind
Rockspire Mountains
Northwind
February 3134; local winter

Will Elliot had seen plenty of pictures of Castle Northwind in his life. The massive gray stone structure was a popular subject for posters and for glossy pictorial volumes about the scenic glories of beautiful Northwind. The tourists he'd used to guide through the northern Rockspires had often been quite put out to learn that the photogenic castle they'd come so far to see was set in the middle of a large expanse of private land and wasn't available to gawk at. He'd certainly never expected to find himself sitting at a table in the castle's lesser hall, drinking tea with the

company Captain and his fellow Sergeants and waiting for word from the Countess.

Lexa McIntosh appeared to agree with him. She
poured more tea into a porcelain cup from the big
silver teapot and added a lump of sugar with the
silver sugar tongs. "It's a long way from Barra Station to a castle in the mountains. Life is good."

"With only three platoons?" Jock Gordon said.
"It's not that good."

Will shook his head. "With three platoons we can
fight off any scouting forays until the main body
arrives."

"That's all very well," the company commander
said, "but just in case the good life decides to give
us some nasty surprises, I want to wire everything
in sight with demolition charges. Starting from the
cliffs by the uphill drive, right the way back to the
public road."

Lexa's gaze drifted over to the windows as the
company commander spoke, and Will saw her eyes
narrow. He followed her glance. The long uphill
drive to the castle's front entrance ran briefly in view
of the windows, but the road when he looked
showed nothing visible, either on the pavement or in
the snowdrifts to either side.

"What was it?" he asked. Lexa had a sharpshoot-
er's keen sight and noticing eye, and if there'd been
something moving on the road a moment before,
she'd have seen it.

"Messenger," she said. "On a fast motorcycle.
None of your damned hoverbikes."

"Looks like the good life's over with," said the

company commander. He set down his tea cup. "I believe that the three of you should go see what the postman has for us today."

Will and his two friends hurried down to the castle's front entrance, arriving in time to stand together on the granite steps as the motorcycle came into view on the last curves of the uphill road. The bike was faster than safe and leaning into the curves so hard that it seemed to be lying on its side. The rider was a man in the uniform of Northwind.

"Message for the company commander," said the messenger.

"Kinda figured that was it," Lexa said. She'd had her laser rifle sighted in on the final curve, and grounded it as she spoke. "Let us have it and we'll carry it up."

The messenger pulled out an envelope with a string seal on it. "I'll need the commander's answer," he said.

"We'll make sure you get it," said Will. He took the envelope. "Wait here. Jock, Lexa—you stay with him."

He carried the sealed envelope back through the castle great hall to the lesser hall where the company commander waited, looking out of the windows at the snowcapped Rockspires and stirring his cup of tea.

"Messenger from central command," Will said with a salute.

"Thanks, Sergeant," the company commander said, returning the salute. He opened the envelope, read the flimsy inside, then put it down. "Please ask the other sergeants to come in. And give this reply to carry back to the Countess and General Griffin. 'We understand.' "

"Sir," Will said, saluted again, and left.

A few minutes later he returned with Jock and Lexa. The company commander, who'd been looking out the window at the Rockspires again, turned around to face them.

"This is where things get interesting," he said. "I've just been given some information, and an order. The information is that the main body of the Highlander force will not be coming here after all. I expect that the reason is this: there's only one way in; there's only one way out. If the main body came here, they could be bottled up by anyone holding the end of the pass.

"The order is very simple. We are to prevent the Steel Wolves from taking Castle Northwind. All means are acceptable. Questions, comments, suggestions, or observations?"

"Blow it up now," Jock said. "With three platoons, we can't hold it."

"We don't want to blow it up until we have to," Will protested. "How about this? Hold it as long as possible, make the Wolves spend time, troops, and matériel, and *then* blow it."

Lexa nodded agreement. "A fight's a fight. Here or somewhere else. If we destroy the castle, and the bad guys don't show up, then we'll have done it all for nothing, and the Countess will be pissed."

"How do you know that?" Jock asked.

"Because if it was me, and it was my castle, *I'd* be pissed."

"I'm thinking much the way you are, Sergeant McIntosh," the company commander said. "But all of the solutions involve the possibility of demolishing this structure at one point or another. So we can start by wiring it. Later, other things. But for right now—"

"Captain," Will asked, "your message. Did it say when the Steel Wolves would get here?"

"Six hours, maybe eight."

"Doesn't matter," Lexa said. "They won't attack until dawn."

"What makes you say that?" the company commander asked.

"Call it intuition. Anastasia Kerensky is a bitch's bitch. She won't stand off and let her troops take our Countess's own castle in the dark—she'll want to be here to watch the flags go down."

"If there's a good chance she'll show up in person—"

"Let me see to my rifle," Lexa said. "If she gets within a mile of me, she's mine."

"Very well," the captain said. "McIntosh, your squad has the road leading in. See to its defenses. Gordon, you have the exterior defenses, as soon as the interior is wired. Elliot, you have interior defense. Help Gordon with the demolition charges, then everyone get some rest. This may be a long night coming."

"Who does he think we are?" Will muttered to Jock as the three sergeants headed down the stairs to give the good word to their platoons. "We already know to sleep every chance we can.

50

"As I came in by Fiddich side, on a May morning. . . ."

Lexa McIntosh hummed under her breath as she lay on the top of a cliff overlooking the road up to Castle Northwind. She was looking to the south, not silhouetted against the sky, invisible to the road, her laser rifle at her shoulder. The large telescopic sight she'd attached to the front of the rifle showed, in great detail, the line of scout vehicles, armor, and infantry moving up the valley toward Castle Northwind. Lexa ignored the scouts and the infantry troopers; she would only have one shot from this position, and she wanted to make the target worth her while.

All right . . . the tank coming into view around the curve was a Condor, with a full-scale Star Colonel—through the telescopic sight she could make out his rank insignia—standing up in the opened top hatch. She tracked him in her sights, a kilometer and a half away, moving at thirty kilometers an hour. If she'd chosen to use one of the Gauss rifles, she'd have had to lead him a bit, so that he and the projectile would arrive at the same point at the same time. With a laser, she didn't need to, and from this point of vantage, on a clear day like today, she didn't need to worry about leaves or fog interfering with the laser's deadly light. Life, she thought, was all about choices, and this one was going to ruin the Star Colonel's day for him.

"Turn again, turn again, turn again I pray ye. . . ."

She took a breath, let half of it out, held what remained. Her finger tightened on the trigger. The laser's beam flashed out like a reddened spear.

"For if ye burn Auchidoon, Huntley he will slay ye."

The Star Colonel twisted and slid down in the hatch of his tank, half of his head burnt away. Lexa closed her eyes, then looked through the sights again. Another vehicle was rounding the bend. The first tank had slowed and turned off the road.

Time to move to another location.

Lexa rolled away from the edge of the cliff, careful not to skyline herself. As soon as she was out of sight from the road, she rose and moved rapidly away. She was still humming.

"As I came in by Fiddich side, on a May morning, Auchidoon was in a blaze, an hour before the dawning."

In her field headquarters at Tara DropPort, Anastasia Kerensky watched the real-time display on the big tri-vid as her troops drove up the road toward Castle Northwind. With the Highlanders now in full retreat out of the city and scattering into the mountains, she had been able to detach a special armored column and give them specific orders: fulfill her angry promise to Tara Campbell by seizing Castle Northwind and claiming it for the Steel Wolves as spoils of war.

Now, in the first light of early morning, the column had reached the cut leading up to the castle. Their progress was relayed back to those watching at headquarters by a camera in the third tank back from the head of the column—progress that in the past few minutes had slowed to a crawl.

"What is the reason for the delay?" Anastasia demanded. "And where is Star Colonel Ulan?"

The face on the video terminal replied, "The Star Colonel is dead, Galaxy Commander."

"What happened?"

"We have been taking sporadic sniper fire, Galaxy Commander."

"Has there been any serious resistance, outside of the sniper fire?"

"None."

"Then carry on."

The Warrior saluted, and shortly afterward the column began moving again. The picture in the headquarters display was impressive, even through the flat pickup from a single camera. The castle lay before them, cradled in its glacial valley, its gray bulk touched with a pink glow from the sun rising beyond the mountain peaks. Tendrils of fog rose from the lake at the castle's foot, and the banners of Northwind and The Republic snapped crisply from the upper towers.

The camera shook as the main gun on the Condor fired.

"Resistance remains light, Galaxy Commander,"

"Good. I want you to capture that castle. In whole. Intact. I have plans for it."

"Galaxy Commander, it shall be done."

No sooner had he spoken than lights twinkled along the side of the northern mountain, among the shadows of the conifers below the timberline. A moment later, geysers of earth rose among the troops and tanks of the advancing Wolves. A volley of short- and medium-range missiles from the armor column's missile carriers replied, departing in a roar like a high wind. A moment later, red fireballs blossomed in the darkness under the trees. "As I said, resistance is—"

The man twitched and fell, blood running from his mouth. For a moment the camera pointed at the ground. Then someone picked it up, and a new man stood in front of the camera.

"Galaxy Commander, this is Star Captain Dane. Star Captain Jothan is now commanding. He asked me to take over this duty. We are about to assault the castle."

Behind Star Captain Dane in the video display, Anastasia could see the scurry of troops heading to the main gate, running in open formation across the field. From either side, over the walls, jump-armored Clan Warriors launched themselves in perfect ballistic trajectories. By the time the running troopers in front had reached the gate, it had been opened for them from within.

"Courtyard, open, light resistance," another voice said, this time with no video accompanying the audio feed. The camera stayed fixed on the castle's exterior, its telephoto lens bringing the far-distant action close to the cameraman's point of view. "Stairway right and left. First squad left, third right. Second squad taking covering position by the door. Moving up reserves, specialists forward. Locked door second level. Setting breaching charges."

The sound of a leaden thud came from the remote audio pickup. An instant later, the same sound came from the microphone held in the field by Star Captain Dane. "Door breached"—the sounds of automatic weapons fire—"room secured. Resistance light. Moving in."

They cleared the castle, room by room. The camera fixed on the castle exterior still showed the banners flying on the parapets. One by one the flags of Northwind came down, and were replaced with the banners of the Steel Wolves.

"Entering final tower," came the audio-pickup voice. "Stairway clear."

An explosion. A different voice continued. "Medics up! Stairway *now* clear. Continuing up. Door. Door is—unlocked. Entering top chamber."

From the field, one Northwind Highland banner

remained, atop a lofty tower, far back in the center of the castle.

"Appears to be a bedchamber. No one present. Here now, what's this?"

The voice inside the castle sounded curious, bemused.

The camera outside showed a light blossoming in that topmost room. The windows filled with light, and the walls expanded. Smoke wreathed the turrets. A noise like thunder, or like surf pounding against cliffs, swept over the field. Smoke, dark and thick, shot through with yellow flames, sprouted where the castle stood. For a moment a castle of fire and light, with walls of smoke, stood against the mist and the mountains. Then it collapsed, with a noise so loud that the microphone could not record it, and in dead silence Castle Northwind vanished.

The camera whipped around, back the way the Steel Wolves had come. From the mouth of the steep valley, between two cliffs, smoke and flame and rock dust were pouring as the mountains on either side were moved together in crumbling avalanches. The camera went back to Star Captain Dane. Blood ran from his nose and ears, a mark of the explosion's concussive force. He moved his mouth, but no sound came out.

Anastasia could read his lips, though: "We're trapped."

She turned away.

"Send troops out into the city," she said. "Have them set fire to everything that can burn. Then all forces gather at the DropPort. Let the Countess of Northwind keep the ruins, if she would sooner turn everything she loves into rubble, rather than have it fall into my hands. We are leaving this cursed planet and taking ship for Terra.

"We are the Warriors that Nicholas Kerensky made for this purpose, and we are going home."

ROC Science Fiction and Fantasy
COMING IN SEPTEMBER 2003

RULED BRITANNIA
by Harry Turtledove
0-451-45915-6

In this alternate England during the Elizabethan era,
William Shakespeare must write a play that will incite the
citizens to rise against the Spanish Monarchy that
rules them.

WAY OF THE WOLF
Book One of The Vampire Earth
by E.E. Knight

0-451-45939-3

Possessed of an unnatural and legendary hunger, the
bloodthirsty Reapers have come to Earth to establish a
New Order built on the harvesting of enslaved human
souls. They rule the planet. They thrive on the scent of fear.
And if it is night, as sure as darkness, they will come.

**Available wherever books are sold, or
to order call: 1-800-788-6262**

Book One of
The Proving Grounds Trilogy

MECHWARRIOR
Dark Age #4
A Silence in the Heavens
By Martin Delrio

From WizKids LLC, creators of the hit game
Mage Knight...

Duchess Tara Campbell and MechWarrior Paladin
Ezekiel Crow struggle to save the planet of
Northwind from the invading faction of
Steel Wolves.

0-451-45932-6

Available wherever books are sold, or
to order call: 1-800-788-6262

R656